The Canyon Castaways

THE CANYON CASTAWAYS

by

Margaret Leighton

FARRAR, STRAUS AND GIROUX
An Ariel Book
NEW YORK

ADVENTURE STORIES

To Nancy Jo and Kathy Anne
with love

The Canyon Castaways

I

As the station wagon sped along the freeway in the heat and fumes of countless other cars, Jill Gray wondered for at least the twentieth time why she hadn't been able to keep herself out of this situation. It was surely the thing she wanted least of all in the world to be doing—to start off on a baby-sitting job in a remote mountain canyon on the very first day of her summer vacation!

For one thing, Jill had always felt shy and nervous with Mrs. Wendell, who was so thin and quick and efficient and who was now driving with such tense concentration through the rush of the traffic. Her long-continued silence and the stiff set of her head and shoulders gave Jill the feeling, too, that Mrs. Wendell was still annoyed by the delay in starting and all the other circumstances which had brought Jill along with them.

The redheaded ten-year-old twins, Peter and Sam, who sat with Jill in the second seat, had always puzzled and baffled her when she had looked after them before. They were very quiet, for boys, and she never knew just what they were thinking. Now they were whispering together and sending seemingly hostile looks in her direction.

Five-year-old Betsey, who was usually so sunny and easygoing, was kneeling on the front seat and staring over its back with round, solemn blue eyes that seemed full of reproach. Jill knew very well that none of the Wendells wanted her along any more than she wanted to be there, and that didn't make things any pleasanter. Only Jody, the black, half-grown cocker spaniel, seemed to be enjoying the trip: he sat with his head out the open window, his long, silky ears lifted by the wind. Every now and then he turned and gave Jill a look that surely could be classed as a smile. Of all the Wendell family he's the only one who likes me as well as he likes Phoebe, Jill told herself. It isn't fair, because the whole thing's Phoebe's fault, not mine. A flood of resentment welled inside her, tightening her throat and making a soreness there which she could not swallow down. And besides all this there was the thought of Rod Campbell to complete her misery.

This day had begun so pleasantly! She had wakened to the familiar smell of bacon and coffee, then sat up in a panic. The hands of the little clock on her bedside table pointed to seven-thirty. I'll have to rush, she thought. Why didn't Mom call me?

Then she had remembered and flung herself back on her pillow. It's vacation, she reminded herself. Summer vacation. I don't have to get up, not ever.

The aroma of the bacon was very enticing, however, and Jill was reaching for her cherry-red robe, when the sound of rushing water halted her. That's Beth in the shower. She'll take hours in there, and I might as well relax.

Jill turned over on her stomach and buried her ruffled brown head in the pillow to shut out the insistent sunlight.

It didn't shut out the silver trilling of a mockingbird in the top of a lemon tree just outside her window, however, nor the smell of frying bacon. She flopped on her back again, linked her fingers under her head, and lay staring at the ceiling.

My first year at Bradley High is over, she thought, and here's the whole summer still untouched, like a Christmas package, all mysterious in its wrappings. What shall I do with this first week, besides sleep late and start reading every book I haven't had time for during the year? Last summer I went to the beach in the mornings. It's so wonderful to get there early, before the crowds arrive, and the big, slow waves follow each other in from all the way across the Pacific—steady, but in no hurry, building into those enormous green, glassy curls that you can see through, before they crest and break. Diving through them is such super fun, and body-surfing, too. Maybe this summer I can learn to use a board.

But who will I go to the beach with, this summer, now that Phoebe won't be here? The question brought a quick frown. I know it's my fault that I haven't made other friends, close friends, at school. But Phoebe's always been right there, just two doors away, and with her around I never seemed to need anyone else.

Jill lay very still, then, pondering a question which had been troubling her for a long time. Am I really such a blank, such a cipher? When I'm alone I make all sorts of plans that seem fine to me, but when I'm with other people their ideas always seem so much better than mine that I follow along with theirs, every time. First it was Beth and Rick whom I tagged after. I suppose little sisters always adore their big sisters and brothers and want to do what they do. I can't remember when I wasn't trying to keep up with them—especially with Rick. Then it was Phoebe.

Phoebe Walker, a year older than Jill, had always been full

5

of projects and enthusiasms, forging ahead with them while Jill followed as best she could. Phoebe won every Girl Scout badge in record time. In junior high she had been all for athletics and was the star at girls' basketball, field hockey, and tennis. She was short and stocky and tireless, while Jill, small-boned and thin and inclined to be dreamy, couldn't keep her pace, no matter how she tried.

Then, in their first week at Bradley High, Phoebe had set herself another goal, and it had changed things for Jill, also. Phoebe had made her announcement while the two were lunching together in the school cafeteria. Jill had been only half-listening to her, for she had been watching the noisy throng of upperclassmen—boys and girls crowding past to their special tables at the end of the big room.

The senior and even the junior girls all seemed to have shining, perfectly-groomed hair done in the latest fashion, and excitingly sophisticated clothes. They wore make-up, which had been strictly forbidden in junior high. As for the senior and junior boys, they were enormous beings who strode through the corridors like bulldozers, scattering everyone before them. They looked right over the heads of the lower classes; even Rick never so much as glanced Jill's way when they passed, especially if he was walking with Rod Campbell.

"What a pair of dreamboats!" Franny Davis, one of Jill's new classmates, had whispered only this morning. "Rick and Rod! The two best-looking boys in the whole school. Rick lives around here, but Rod's from the South. They say he has the most marvelous, romantic line with girls!"

When Jill had told her that Rick was her own brother, Franny had practically swooned. "Then I suppose you know Rod real well, too?" she had asked, enviously.

"Not very," Jill had answered, which was a good deal less than the truth. She had never so much as met him, although to her mind he far outranked any movie star in good looks.

6

Rick and his school friends might have inhabited another planet so far as his young sister was concerned.

Then Phoebe's next words had jolted Jill suddenly back to the cafeteria again. "And so I've made up my mind. I'm going to be a doctor," Phoebe said.

"A doctor!" Jill had exclaimed, her tuna sandwich halted halfway to her mouth. "But that takes years and years. You'll have to go to the University and then to medical school after that!"

"That's right. And to do all that I'll have to make top grades here at Bradley because I'll have to get a scholarship if I expect to go to the University. My folks can't afford to send me unless I do, even with all the money I can earn baby-sitting between now and then. So what I'm going to do from now on, Jill, is to get the highest grades in the whole class. You wait and see! I think I'll even plan to be a surgeon. I'm good at biology—I don't mind cutting up frogs, even when they kick."

"But a surgeon would have to cut up people!" Jill protested. "That would be different. My goodness, Phoebe, I don't believe I want to be a doctor. Truly I don't."

Phoebe had looked at her then, crinkling up her eyes in the way she had when she was teasing. "Well, Jill, if you don't want to you truly don't have to," she said. "You're a big girl now. You aren't obliged to tag after me forever, you know."

Sometimes Phoebe rubbed it in pretty hard that she was always the leader. Jill felt color rising in her cheeks and she lifted her chin. "That's right, I'm not," she answered. "I guess I've been doing it too long, already. I suppose, too, you think I couldn't get good enough grades, anyway?"

Phoebe's smile had faded then, and she looked sorry. "Oh, Jill, you have as good a brain as I have—maybe better. Your only trouble is that you haven't any confidence in yourself.

7

I've always thought it was because you're the youngest in your family and the others have always decided everything for you—sort of babied you, to tell the truth. You could do anything—and I mean *anything*—if you ever wanted it hard enough. If you wanted to be a doctor, you'd manage it."

"Well, I happen not to want to," Jill had answered, her cheeks redder than ever. Did Phoebe think she was making things any better by calling her a baby?

This small spat hadn't lasted long and they were soon good friends again, but Phoebe's decision had made a change. At school they had seen less and less of each other. Phoebe now hurried through her lunch hour and then went to the library to study, and Jill was often left alone. A group of her new classmates had tried to draw her into their circle, but Jill had never felt really comfortable with them. They were gay and lively and prettily dressed and they all knew a lot more than she did about clothes and hair-dos, make-up and manicures, which meant absolutely nothing to Phoebe. And boys—especially boys! When they talked and giggled and whispered about them Jill, who had never had a date in her life, felt wretchedly childish and ignorant.

When they introduced Jill to the boys who joined them at recess they always said, "This is Rick Gray's sister." None of the boys paid much attention to Jill, however, and she was never included in groups going to the beach on Saturdays or to the movies. Not one of those boys seemed interesting or attractive enough to Jill, anyway, to cause all the excitement the other girls seemed to feel. Now, if one of them had been Rod Campbell . . . !

Thinking back over the year as she lay in bed that morning, Jill had turned her head uneasily on the pillow. I guess I really didn't fit in with them, she decided. They were nice to me only because I'm Rick's sister, not because of me at all.

The year hasn't been very happy. To tell the honest truth, it's often been lonely.

Even after school Phoebe had worked whenever she could at baby-sitting. She was very good at it and was much in demand, and any plans she and Jill might make were always subject to cancellation if one of her "clients" called on her. She had asked Jill to act as her substitute several times, when two requests conflicted, so that she could keep her list intact. This summer Phoebe had taken a full-time job and would be going to the mountains this very day with the Wendell family. Jill herself had substituted with them two or three times. Mrs. Wendell scared her a little, but the kids were okay.

Just at this point Beth had put her becurlered head through Jill's bedroom door. "The shower's free, Jilly-baby," she called. A pleasant smell of bath oils lingered in the hallway behind her, where Jill paused for a moment to see if Rick wanted the shower. He was always annoyed if he had to wait for anyone, especially for her. His door stood open, however, and she could hear him whistling somewhere downstairs. I wonder why he's up so early this morning, the first day of vacation, she thought idly as she turned on the water and held her face up to the warm, liquid rush.

Out of the shower, and dry, she felt more cheerful as she rummaged through her closet for something especially vacationy to wear. She found the yellow shorts and the top with the big red-and-yellow hibiscus blossoms printed on it that she had liked last summer. They were both a little snug for her now, but she could still get into them. She combed back her damp, curly brown hair, tied it with a yellow ribbon, and went down to breakfast feeling very gay and festive.

Her father had gone to work already—his place was cleared and empty. She could hear her mother moving about in the kitchen, although her usual second cup of coffee, already

9

poured, stood by her plate. Beth and Rick were still seated at the table and there, in the chair beside Jill's, sat Rod Campbell finishing a plate of bacon and eggs! Rod Campbell, blond and handsome as a Greek god, who not only stood up when she appeared but held her chair for her as though she were a duchess, or at least a senior girl, and at the same time gave a soft, low, admiring whistle.

"Rick, you dog!" he said. "You've been hiding things from me. Why didn't you tell me you had *two* such absolute knockouts for sisters?"

Jill had felt herself blushing with pleasure, although she realized at the same moment that it wasn't too flattering to be told that she hadn't been noticed at all for a whole year at high school! However, she couldn't say that without sounding ungracious. She was drawing in her breath to attempt a reply when Beth broke in.

"Isn't he wonderful, Jill? You can always count on these Southern boys to compliment the ladies. Rick, you could really learn a lot from Rod," she said.

"Learn from him? That'll be the day!" Rick said, with a loud guffaw.

Then Mrs. Gray had come in through the swinging door of the kitchen, bringing a plate piled high with fresh-baked biscuits. "Good morning, Jill-baby," she said. "I thought perhaps you'd sleep late, so I haven't squeezed any orange juice for you yet. How are you, darling?" She dropped a kiss on the top of Jill's head as she placed the biscuits before the boys. Beth had inherited her mother's golden blondness and also her tendency to plumpness, while Rick and Jill were thin and dark like their father, with his black-lashed, hazel eyes.

"I'm fine, Mom. I'll squeeze my own juice. You sit down and drink your coffee," Jill said.

"Beth's been away at college and that explains why I hadn't met her before this. But what about this other gorgeous creature? Jill—is that your name, sugar? Where have they been hiding *you*?" Rod asked.

"I'll tell him for you, Jelly Bean. He really deserves it," Rick said, grinning. "She's been passing you in the corridor every day for the last ten months. In other words, she's just finished her first year at good old Bradley."

Rod looked a little abashed then, but only for an instant. He struck his brow with a dramatic gesture. "So that's what's been haunting me all this time! I knew there was something. You see, it's a strict rule among us upper classmen not even to *look* at freshman girls, but somehow, through that invisible wall, I sensed that I was missing something. It was *you*! Well, summer's come and we can remedy that, beginning right now. Beth's already broken my heart by saying that she's engaged to some college jerk, but maybe you can mend it. What are you doing this morning? Will you come surfing with Rick and me? I think you're just the type I'd like to share my surfboard with."

"Oh, I'd *love* to!" Jill cried, hardly daring to believe what she had heard. Ever since Rick had become such an expert surfer Jill had begged and begged him to teach her, but he had always dismissed the idea scornfully. "I can be ready in a minute," she added.

Rick's teasing grin changed to a black-browed frown. "Hold it! I have something to say about this—it's my car, remember. I've made plans for us to go down to Mariners' Cove and meet the bunch there. I'm to pick up three other guys on the way. We've agreed not to bring any girls along, to say nothing of kid sisters!"

Rod had lifted his shoulders and spread his hands in a helpless shrug. "There we are—foiled again. But never mind, there're other days coming, Jill. The whole, long, golden summer lies ahead. This is only the beginning."

"Except that you're going north the end of the week to

begin your vacation job, remember?" Rick said. "Don't be-lieve a word he says, Jelly Bean—it's only his line. Come along, Don Juan, surf's up and we're missing a lot of good waves. Let's get going."

"Another time, then. I mean it," Rod said, getting to his feet and pushing back his chair. "I'll call you later in the week. We can have at least one good date before I go. Okay, Jill?"

"Okay," Jill answered. Rod thanked Mrs. Gray for the breakfast, and the boys departed. Jill had managed a smile and a wave of her hand which she hoped looked gay and casual, but disappointment was hot within her. She hurried into the kitchen and began to squeeze her orange juice, while the sound of Rick's noisy motor died in the distance. She cut through the oranges with vicious slashes of the knife and pressed down so hard on the handle of the squeezer that some of the juice spurted out and hit her in the eye. Rick could have let me come, she told herself, dabbing at the stinging liquid. He was really mean. I'm a good swimmer—I wouldn't have been in the way. He didn't have to call me "Jelly Bean," either—not in front of Rod. And no matter what Rick said, I think Rod really meant it when he said he'd call me for a date. A date with Rod Campbell! The thought was almost too dazzling to bear.

She had come back into the dining room with the full glass in her hand when the doorbell rang. "I'll go," she said, set the glass on the table, and ran to the door.

2

At the door stood Mrs. Walker, Phoebe's mother, anxious and out of breath. "Oh Jill, I'm so glad you're here!" she exclaimed. "Something terrible has happened. Phoebe tripped going downstairs early this morning and hurt herself. Her father took her to the doctor, and the doctor says she's fractured a bone in her arm. She's in the hospital now getting it set."

"In the hospital!" Jill was echoing when her mother pushed past her.

"Why Jill-baby, don't leave Mrs. Walker standing out here. Come in, Edith, and sit down," she urged, putting an arm about her friend. "Here, have a cup of coffee. What a shame, and just when Phoebe was planning to start her wonderful summer job too!"

"That's why I came over here, Clara," Mrs. Walker said, sinking into a chair. "Your coffee does smell good. My goodness, I've been so upset I haven't had any yet—it's been such a dreadful morning! You know how Phoebe is when she sets her mind on something, and she really counted on this job. Mrs. Wendell may be a little strict and demanding, but she pays well and she likes Phoebe. Their cabin is up in a remote little canyon on the side of a mountain. It's a lovely spot, they say, but so far that Professor Wendell can only get there on weekends while he's teaching summer school. He doesn't want Mrs. Wendell to be alone there with only the children, such a long way from civilization."

"I can understand that," Mrs. Gray nodded.

"Well, Phoebe just telephoned me from the hospital. She's really a wonderful girl, if I do say so myself, Clara, the way she's kept her head through everything. Even in all that pain, she was thinking clearly. Mrs. Wendell had arranged to pick her up at eight this morning, and Phoebe had already called her to tell her about the accident."

"That *was* thoughtful of Phoebe," Jill's mother said. "Mrs. Wendell will have to postpone going, of course."

"Well, no." Mrs. Walker hesitated, then continued, "Mrs. Wendell doesn't like to change her plans—she's so very well organized, always. She told Phoebe that she'd have to get someone else to take her place, another high school girl who had asked for the job. But the trouble is this other girl will come today only if it's for the whole summer, not for just the week or so that Phoebe will be incapacitated."

"Oh, what a shame!" Jill cried. "Then Phoebe's whole summer's job will be lost. She'll have to look for another. That's not fair."

"No, it doesn't seem fair to me, either," Mrs. Walker agreed, nodding at Jill, then turning back to her mother. "But Phoebe wouldn't give up so easily and she was ready with an idea—a plan Mrs. Wendell has agreed to. Phoebe suggested that Jill go up to the cabin with the Wendells this morning and substitute for Phoebe, just the way she has before, until

Phoebe's able to function again. Would you agree to let Jill go, Clara? Mrs. Wendell says she must start no later than ten o'clock. I know it's very short notice, but Jill could use Phoebe's camping blankets and some of her clothes if she needs them. Getting her ready wouldn't be too much of a problem. It would mean everything to Phoebe—everything!"

"Why . . ." Mrs. Gray hesitated only a moment. "I don't see why not. The Wendells are very reliable people, and Jill has been with them before. Yes, surely. You can be ready by ten, can't you, baby?"

Jill's head was whirling. But what about *me?* she was thinking. Is this all to be decided without even asking me whether or not I want to go? Then another thought came to her and her heart gave a dreadful downward plunge. And what about my date with Rod?

Something of all this must have shown in her face, for Beth was eying her sharply. "What's the matter, Jill? Aren't you going to say anything? Phoebe's your best friend. You do want to help her out, don't you?"

"Of course she does," their mother said, brushing the question aside. "Jill will be only too glad to do anything she can to help, Edith. Won't you, darling? Any little plans she may have made for this week can be easily postponed."

When it had been put to her so directly, Jill could only nod assent. "Yes, of course," she had managed to say. She hadn't made any plans at all, actually. There was only the single, small but oh-so-bright-and-shining hope that Rod Campbell would telephone and ask her for a date. And with it was the darkly looming fact that he was leaving at the end of the week. If I lose this chance I may never have another again, ever. But how can I explain this to everyone now, she thought in despair, and was silent.

Even now, speeding along in the Wendells' car, Jill didn't see how she could have managed differently. By this time, they had at last traversed the city and all its suburbs. The freeway was less crowded as it carried them eastward over the flat landscape where nothing grew among the sand and rocks but sagebrush and greasewood and some scattered cactus. Before them loomed the wall of mountains, their bases hidden by a purplish-brown haze of heat and smog, their upper slopes covered with mesquite that looked like folds of dark green velvet. It was hot and getting hotter every minute. The twins' faces were flushed under their freckles, little Betsey's cheeks were crimson, and Jody panted audibly. Nobody had spoken for a long time.

"Aren't we going to stop for lunch?" Peter asked, at last. "I'm hungry—and thirsty, too."

"There are some sandwiches in that paper bag and there's water in the Thermos jug," Mrs. Wendell told him in her crisp, definite voice. "With all the delay in getting started, I don't want to take time out to stop and eat. We must get there before sunset. You know how quickly the dark comes in our canyon, and the last part of the road is the worst. Give Jody some dog biscuits and some water in his dish."

Peanut butter sandwiches weren't too appetizing in the heat, even with cold water to wash them down. Jill could manage only a few bites of hers, but the twins and Betsey munched doggedly until theirs were gone, then finished Jill's share, too.

"I wish the car radio was working," Sam said.

"Phoebe always sang songs to us when there wasn't anything to look at," Betsey said. "Sing something, Jill."

"What would you like me to sing?" Jill asked, her mind all at once blank and empty of any tunes at all.

" 'Frog Went A-Courtin',' " Betsey answered promptly, then settled down in expectant silence with her chin on the back of the front seat.

After a squeaky beginning, for her throat was dry again

from the heat, Jill launched self-consciously upon such verses of the old song as she could remember. The twins listened solemnly for a while, then turned away to the window, as did Jody, all three preferring the bare, sun-scorched landscape to Jill's efforts.

When she had finished, Betsey shifted her position. "You aren't such a very good singer, are you Jill? Phoebe knows *all* the verses, every single word," she said. "But thank you, anyway."

At last the car was turning off the freeway and heading directly toward the great rocky barrier. "There's the road up to our canyon—that white scar along the side of the mountain," Sam said, pointing.

Now that they had changed direction and seemed at last to be making some progress toward their goal, the children's spirits revived. They began to chatter about the place and their experiences in previous years. "It's really keen there," Peter said. "We're the only people in the whole canyon. There used to be other cabins but a winter flood washed all the rest of them out and they never were rebuilt, and then Dad bought the whole place. There's nothing beyond us but deer trails and fire roads. There used to be an old gold mine on the side of the mountain just above us—there's still a trail going up to it. There isn't any gold there, though. Dad says there never was much, but it belongs to us, anyway."

"The canyon's full of trees, lots of cedar and hemlock and even some big pines. There's a stream with two waterfalls, one above us and one below us, and basins carved out of the rock by the water big enough to lie and float in, with ferns all around them, and there's a trout pool, way up beyond. Lots of birds, too. I brought my bird book and I'm going to keep a record of all I see," Sam added.

"There's squirrels and darling little chipmunks, too," Betsey chimed in.

17

"Yes, and deer, scads of deer. Almost too many, the ranger says," Peter announced. "Last year he saw some mountain lion tracks only a little way from our cabin. Do you like mountain lions, Jill?"

"Goodness, of course not!" Jill said, surprised at the question. "They kill deer and calves and young colts, don't they? I think they're dreadful."

"That's where you're mistaken," Peter declared importantly. "Phoebe says that mountain lions are *good*, because they help to maintain the balance of nature." He waited a moment to note the effect this news had on Jill, then went on. "What she meant was that, where there aren't any mountain lions and the deer are protected by law, why, there get to be just too many deer. Then they eat off all the groundcover, and when the rains come there's nothing left growing to hold the water in the soil, so there's a flood. It washes the good dirt down the mountainsides until, before long, it's all barren, like desert. The ranger said that she was right and it's something that all of them worry about a lot," he finished in triumph.

"Is that so?" Jill said, too genuinely interested to resent this further proof of Phoebe's superiority. "Still, I wouldn't like to meet a mountain lion all of a sudden, anyway."

"That's another myth, the ranger says," Sam stated. "Mountain lions aren't a bit vicious. They don't attack people. Besides, you aren't likely to see one, anyway. They're very shy and they make less noise for their size than any other creature in the woods. You never even hear them."

"Well *that's* a relief, anyway," Jill said.

"*I* think it would be wonderful to see one," Peter said, "I'm going to look for their tracks all summer. If I see any tracks I'm going to lie in wait beside them every night with a camera and flashbulbs until I get a picture of one. I have a camera, you know, and I got the flash attachment for it for

Christmas. Phoebe was going to teach me how to take night pictures, and if I got some good ones she would have entered them in some contest she knows about. I might have won a big prize."

"She still can teach you, of course. She won't be laid up all summer, you know. It will be only a week or so before she's able to come here," Jill told him.

"Thank goodness for *that*!" Sam said.

Peter turned upon him. "O, shut up!" he admonished. "That's impolite. It's not Jill's fault that she's not—what I mean is, she'll do the best she can, like Mom said, and we mustn't crab about it, no matter how we feel."

This backhanded defense, or whatever it was meant to be, suddenly struck Jill as so funny that she began to laugh, and her laughter seemed to clear the air. The boys chuckled uncertainly, too, and Betsey joined in with a giggle. Everyone seemed all at once in better spirits. They had reached the foothills at last and had begun to climb, and the heat had decreased noticeably.

At a place where the road forked stood a solitary building, evidently a store and gas station. "That's the Cedar Bend store. It belongs to Mr. Garrett," Sam said.

There was no one in sight, except a man who sat on the porch of the store fast asleep, his chair tipped back against the wall and his hat over his eyes. "There's Mr. Garrett now," Peter cried. "Aren't we going to stop and buy something, Mom?"

"Not this time. We're late already, and you know how he talks. We wouldn't get away from him until dark," his mother said as they spun past.

Betsey turned to look back. "He hasn't waked up. I'm glad he didn't see us go by without even saying hello. I think it would have hurt his feelings."

They took the less traveled of the two forks and soon were

winding upward along the banks of a dry wash that was full of boulders, with a few scanty puddles here and there. "This is the lower end of our creek. It doesn't look like much here, but wait until you see it higher up," Sam said.

As they climbed, the road grew narrower and rougher, and the car had to proceed slowly. It skirted close beside what, after a while, became an actually flowing stream edged with willows whose sun-warmed scent was sweet in the nostrils. On and on, for more than an hour by Jill's watch. Several times jack rabbits ran ahead of them in the ruts of the road before deciding to leap off into the brush, and once a chapparal cock, or road runner, paced them with its queer, ungainly stride. "They fight rattlers and kill them, too," Peter said as the bird finally disappeared into a thicket. "I'd like to see one do it, just once."

"Are there many rattlers up here?" Jill asked uneasily, while within her she felt the familiar cold, crawling horror the mere mention of the creatures invariably brought on.

"Some. We always watch out for them, and Mom keeps a snake kit handy," Sam told her. "But there aren't any right around our cabin—only up among the rocks and sagebrush. Why? Are you afraid of them?"

"Of course I am. Isn't everybody?" Jill demanded.

"Not Phoebe. Phoebe isn't scared of anything," Betsey stated.

They were now driving through a more open part of the canyon, and soon they passed a neatly fenced forest ranger station with its flags blowing in the breeze. "The ranger's name is Jim. He's a real nice guy," Sam said. "I guess he's out on his rounds. I don't see his truck anywhere."

Then the road grew still steeper and rougher. Mrs. Wendell drove expertly, but even so the wheels often skidded jarringly over loose rocks that had fallen from the canyon walls. "Gosh,

I hope the road's okay this year through the narrow gorge," Sam said. "It's always worst of all there."

"Your father came over it two weeks ago when he drove up to bring our supplies," his mother said. "He reported that it was rough but passable. Don't worry."

The canyon walls were now so high that they shut out all but a strip of blue sky. From time to time they rattled over wooden bridges from which they could look down into what was now a foaming, rushing torrent of bright water. Ferns grew out of the crevices in the mossy rocks; cedar trees, dark hemlocks, ruddy-trunked pines lined the stream. Jill breathed deeply, drawing in the rich forest scent. It's really lovely here, she thought. I might almost enjoy it if—if things were different!

They rounded a sharp bend and Mrs. Wendell braked the car suddenly. "Look!" she whispered.

In the middle of the road a deer and a fawn stood still as statues for the barest instant before they went bounding up the steep slope in great, feather-light leaps. "Oh, how marvelous! How beautiful!" Jill cried aloud, her heart leaping with them.

"You'll get used to them," Sam said. "They're all around our cabin early every morning."

Blue shadows were already beginning to gather in the depths of the canyon, although the sky overhead was still bright, when they crossed another bridge over a plunging waterfall, made a last turn, and drew to a halt. "There it is!" Peter cried. "There's our place."

The boys and Betsey and Jody, too, were out of the car as soon as it stopped, running everywhere at once like four unleashed puppies. Jill sat for another moment trying to take it all in. It's like a picture in my old fairy-tale book, she thought. This little open glade in the forest, with the long tree shadows crossing it and that low-roofed log hut looking so tiny under the great pines. It might be the cottage where the woodcutter's daughter was living when the prince came riding by with his hawks and his hounds. Or Snow White and Rose Red. Beyond, through a screen of willows, she could see what looked like a tall white pillar, except that it kept shifting and shimmering. Then, when the car's engine stopped, the sound of the second waterfall came rushing to meet her.

"It *is* a pretty place, isn't it?" Mrs. Wendell said, her tense, tired face softening. "Well, we'd better begin to unload. The dark comes very quickly, here."

She was taking down the tail gate of the station wagon when Peter and Sam came running back to them, their eyes round. "There's a car there," Sam said. "A jeep, at the foot of the trail that goes up to our gold mine."

3

"A jeep?" Mrs. Wendell echoed. "It must belong to the ranger."

"No," Sam shook his head. "I know Jim's truck. This is a jeep, and besides it's a lot dirtier and more beat-up than anything he'd ever drive. Come and see."

Mrs. Wendell, Jill, Betsey, and Jody, too, crossed the clearing to where the car stood, in the shade of a clump of willows. "Well, it certainly is 'beat-up' looking, as you say," Mrs. Wendell agreed. "I wonder whose it is. Probably one of the neighboring rancher's."

"We can tell by the registration," Jill said. The card had evidently been rained on at some time, however, and she couldn't read the blurred printing. "It was left here only a little while ago, though. The twigs and leaves that were broken when it drove under the willows are still fresh."

"Well, let's get back to our unpacking," Mrs. Wendell said.

"But wait, Mom. What's it doing on our property?" Sam demanded.

Mrs. Wendell smiled. "Why, Sam, this isn't the city. There's no reason why anyone shouldn't park here. There's plenty of room."

"Yes, but I'd sure like to know who it is, anyway." Peter's eyes suddenly brightened with excitement. "I bet he's looking for gold in our gold mine!"

Mrs. Wendell shook her head impatiently. "Your father would say that he's welcome to any he can find," she told him. "You know he had the place looked over by a geologist, and he said whatever gold was there was worked out a long time ago."

"I think it's very mysterious, anyway," Peter insisted.

"Look! Here are the footprints of whoever it was, going up the old trail," Sam cried. "There were two men. One of them had great big feet and the other wore sneakers. New sneakers. He made prints just like ours, only bigger."

"Let's follow them and see what they're doing," Peter said.

"Not now, boys. I need you to help carry in the bedding and clothes and put the supplies away. Then you must bring in a pail of water and gather wood for the fireplace before it gets too dark to see. Whoever it is will surely be coming down again as soon as the light's gone," his mother told him.

Reluctantly, the twins set to work unloading the rolls of blankets and the suitcases from the station wagon. Mrs. Wendell unlocked the door, and Jill, her arms full, followed her inside. The interior was warm from being closed up, but it had a pleasant, woodsy smell, anyway. It consisted of a single big room, with red-curtained bunks along two sides, a fireplace, and a lean-to which housed the kitchen.

"No electricity and no plumbing," Mrs. Wendell announced, cheerfully. "The toilet's that little edifice on the hillside among those cedars. We get our water from the stream and bathe and wash there, too. We burn wood in the fireplace to keep warm when it gets chilly in the evenings, and we burn special fuel in the Coleman lamps and the cooking stove. Now let me see. I'd better get a lamp filled and lit before dark."

The kitchen shelves were stocked with enough cans, jars, and packages to last all summer, Jill thought. Mrs. Wendell looked them over quickly, then began a more careful survey. "Now where in the world . . ." she murmured, annoyance in her voice. "You'd think George would have put the cans of Coleman fuel in plain sight. I wonder—perhaps he didn't want to leave them inside the cabin because of fire or something. But where could they be?"

A thorough search of the house, the shed, even the outhouse, failed to show the missing cans. By this time, dusk was really gathering. "We have our flashlights," Sam said. "Why can't we use them instead of the lamp?"

"We'll have to, tonight, of course, but we can't cook with them," Mrs. Wendell almost snapped. "Well, it's no use. How provoking of George, when I gave him such a careful list! Well, I should have known better than to rely on him. He probably mislaid my list at the first place he stopped. He's a very brilliant man in his field, but he can be absent-minded. It really seems to me that nothing gets done properly in this family unless I do it myself! Have you brought the wood in, boys?"

"Can't we cook over the fireplace?" Peter asked. "We can broil hot dogs there, anyhow, and they taste a lot better than fried on the stove, I think."

"That's what we'll have to do tonight, at least," his mother said. "But I must make that long trip down to the store for fuel in the morning. What a bother!"

"Then you will have to buy something from nice Mr. Garrett, after all!" Betsey said with delight, to which her mother made no answer.

The boys soon brought in a stack of wood, and Jill set herself to building the fire in the big stone fireplace, thankful that she remembered how from her days as a Girl Scout. "At least Dad didn't forget the matches," Peter said, watching her work.

"You build fires just the way Phoebe does," Sam commented. "And almost as well."

"Don't forget our water. Get it while you can still see," Mrs. Wendell reminded them, and the boys went out swinging the big galvanized pail between them. "Oh, and while you're there, take your jackknives and cut some green willow sticks to hold our hot dogs."

The twins were gone so long that Mrs. Wendell sent Jill out to see what was keeping them. She met them coming down the trail from the old mine. "We went up a little way to see if we could find those men," Sam explained. "They didn't go all the way up to the mine, though. They turned off along the fire road."

"Well, our fire's ready for the wieners, and the rest of us are hungry. Suppose you get the water and the willow sticks," Jill told them. "Those men are probably just hikers, back-packing into the mountains."

The roasted hot dogs were delicious. With powdered milk beaten up in cold creek water, canned string beans, a salad of lettuce and tomatoes brought along that day and still fresh— if a trifle on the warm side—and cookies for dessert, everyone ate heartily. "But I would like a good cup of coffee," Mrs. Wendell sighed.

"We could heat water over the coals and use instant coffee, if you have some," Jill suggested.

Mrs. Wendell made a face. "I can't abide that stuff, and I didn't bring any. I hate to put my good percolator over a wood fire, too, so I'll just have to wait until tomorrow. Maybe I'll sleep all the better without it."

They all went to bed early, for everyone was tired. Betsey

was half asleep when Jill buttoned her into her pajamas and tucked her into her bunk, but the boys were reluctant at first. They yawned so widely, even in the middle of protesting, however, that their mother sent them up into their bunks without further argument.

Jill lay awake watching through the red curtains of her bunk as the embers in the fireplace faded to ashes. There had been so much to do in getting settled that she hadn't had time to think of the events of the morning, but now they returned to her in an unhappy flood. That Rod Campbell should ask her for a date still seemed to her the most wonderful event of her whole life. Then to have to come away, up into these remote mountains, when he was leaving at the end of the week! It was almost too cruel to be borne!

If only Rick had let me go along with them to the beach, Jill thought, I'd have been off and away before Mrs. Walker ever came over. But then—but then—? Phoebe would have missed her whole summer's job. I wouldn't have wanted that, of course. But why should Phoebe's affairs always be so much more important than mine? she found herself thinking rebelliously, and that lump was there in her throat again.

The night had seemed very still at first, except for the constant soft rush of the waterfalls. Then, as Jill grew more accustomed to what had seemed silence, she could distinguish other sounds. Although there was very little breeze, there was a continuous low-pitched murmur in the pines above the cabin, sleepy birdcalls, frogs in the stream—and tree frogs, too —the endless rhythmic rasp of night insects, minute stirrings of leaves and brush. At intervals, from a long distance, the eerie yipping of coyotes reached her. Once, just as she was dozing off, a screech owl brought her awake again, making her quiver with fright until she realized what it was. A forest is a noisy place, she thought, and fell asleep at last.

Jill found herself awake again when dawn was still only a

vague grayness in the room. It had grown so much warmer that she was perspiring, and she threw back her covers. Then came a low, distant rumbling. That's thunder, she thought. It's still a long way off, thank goodness. I hope we don't have a storm. I hate thunder and lightning, especially in the mountains. There was no more of it, however, and she slept again.

The morning was bright and cloudless, so far as they could tell from their limited view of the sky. Everyone had slept late, and there was an oppressive, close feeling in the air that increased as the sun grew warmer.

"Well, I suppose I simply must go down for those cans of fuel," Mrs. Wendell said, at last. "I hate to start, because it's going to be a disagreeably hot drive. I think you children will be better off here than coming with me."

"I'd rather stay here, anyway," Betsey said, "even though I'd like to see nice Mr. Garrett. There's a chipmunk in the woodpile and I'm going to coax him out. Last summer we had one so tame that he ate from our hands, remember?"

"I'd rather stay here, too, and build a dam so we can set up our water wheel, as we planned before," Sam said, and he and Peter rushed out of doors and down to the stream.

"It will take me some time to go down and back, Jill," Mrs. Wendell said as she got into the station wagon. "You can give the children their lunch. Better make sandwiches and use up what bread is left before it dries out altogether. You know how to mix up the instant milk powder, of course. They can have apples and cookies, too." She started the engine, then put her head out of the window. "You aren't worried about that jeep and whoever it belongs to, are you? I'm perfectly sure it's one of the nearby ranchers and that they've left it here while they're out looking for stray cattle or horses. The boys have to have their mystery, though, especially Peter."

"Oh, I'm not worried," Jill answered, smiling as brightly as she could. Until this moment she hadn't been, but now the thought of being alone in charge of the children with this question still unsolved was suddenly a little dismaying.

"Good girl!" Mrs. Wendell said. "I keep forgetting that you aren't Phoebe and that I shouldn't expect as much from you. I always knew that she could cope with anything and I never had a moment's uneasiness when she was here. The only real danger, as of course you know, is from rattlers. You saw where we keep the snake-bite kit, remember? The directions on it are very simple and clear. But the children have been constantly warned to watch out for them, so there's practically no chance at all of their being bitten. Well, I must get started. The sooner I go the sooner I'll be back."

Jill watched her drive around the turn and heard the car rattle over the bridge above the waterfall. *Rattlesnakes!* That same cold, sick shivering began again inside her. She had never admitted to anyone how great was her terror of the reptiles, and of course she couldn't now. Yet how could Mrs. Wendell speak so calmly about the possibility of her children being bitten? I do know where the snake-bite kit is, and I do remember being shown how to use it in Girl Scouts, but could I ever slice into someone's flesh with a razor blade, as it says to do? What if I tried and did it wrong—cut an artery, for instance? Or what if I fainted dead away at first sight of the horrible creature and so was no use at all?

A rustling in the pine needles behind her brought her heart to a thudding stop. Hardly daring to stir, she turned her head slowly, slowly. . . . It was only a small green lizard, however, and Jill's relief was so vast that she gasped aloud. Well, there's no use standing here and scaring myself to death. I'd better do something—clean up after our breakfast, first of all, she decided.

Since there was no hot water, Jill took the few dishes and cups down to the creek and scoured them with sand. Dabbling in the clear, cold water was pleasant, especially since the air had this heavy, breathless quality. A little farther downstream the twins' red heads were bent above the rocks they were hauling into place to build their dam. Betsey was still waiting patiently beside the woodpile for the chipmunk to emerge, a piece of bread in her hand.

Jody came nosing up to Jill, whining. "What's the matter? You've had your breakfast," Jill said, rubbing his soft ears. Jody allowed himself to be caressed but kept up his queer, unhappy whimpering. "Perhaps you wanted to go in the car? It'll be back soon," she assured him.

When she came back into the cabin to make up the bunks, Jody still kept close beside her, so close that Jill almost tripped over him several times. Another roll of thunder echoed from somewhere and she went out to look at the sky again. It certainly feels like a storm's coming, but I can't see a cloud anywhere, she said to herself. There's so little of the sky to see, though, down in this canyon. There are probably clouds farther up or maybe just around the side of the mountain, but so long as they aren't overhead it can't rain on us. That's for sure, she decided.

Betsey had given up waiting for the chipmunk and was now busily doling out crumbs to two beautiful, deep-blue mountain jays, "camp robbers" as the miners called them. They were unbelievably bold, and before long they were eating out of the little girl's hand, pausing often to scold each other and her with raucous squawks when one got more than seemed his share.

There were a great many fresh deer tracks around the cabin, too. If I had wakened early enough I could have seen them, Jill thought. I'll try not to sleep so late tomorrow. She went back into the cabin, found a broom, and swept the floor, then dusted the whole place. If Mom could see me now, she'd be surprised, she thought, for housework wasn't Jill's strong point.

The exertion had made her warmer than ever. She went outside, hoping to cool her hot face, but the outdoors was equally close and warm. I don't remember ever before feeling this way in the mountains, she said to herself. It's really suffocating. Even the birds are quiet.

Jody, close at her heels always, whined again and looked up pleadingly into her face. "It's all right, little doggie," she told him. "Just hot weather—and, of course, there's the altitude! I'd forgotten all about that and how it makes you feel when you first come up from sea level. That's why the heat bothers me so much, and I suppose it affects Jody, too.

This seemed a reassuring explanation, and Jill was breathing a small sigh of relief when suddenly another roll of thunder, longer, louder, and more continuous, rumbled through the canyon. Oh dear, I hope it doesn't rain until Mrs. Wendell gets back, Jill thought, frowning. Rain could make that road really bad. She looked anxiously at her watch. No, she can't even have got down out of the narrow part of the canyon yet, she figured.

The children seemed unworried by the thunder. The twins had looked up from their work briefly but now paid no further attention. Betsey brushed the crumbs from her hands. "That's all I have for you," she told the blue jays. "Fly away home to your families." The jays, however, continued to screech indignantly and to flutter about her. "You're certainly not very polite guests, even if you are pretty," she added, severely. "When will we have lunch, Jill?"

"Pretty soon," Jill said. "What kind of sandwiches do you want, boys?"

"Peanut butter," they answered, practically in unison.

"I want peanut butter, too, but with jelly on it," Betsey said.

"I'll bring it out and we can eat over there under that big pine by the stream," Jill said. "That is, if it doesn't rain."

"It won't rain," Sam stated positively. "It thunders a lot up here, but all the rain falls on the other side of the mountain."

Jill spread the sandwiches, piled them on a paper plate in a gay Mexican basket she found, beat the powdered milk with water in a plastic pitcher, and set it, with some plastic cups, the apples, and the cookies, carefully in the basket, too. When she stepped outside with it the sun was still shining, but the edge of a dark thunderhead had appeared in the patch of blue sky above them. She hesitated a moment, listening. There was a new sound in the air that was not thunder.

"It's a plane!" Peter cried.

No, it wasn't a plane, nor thunder, but a new and different sound altogether, and it was growing rapidly louder. What was it? It was accompanied by a kind of vibration that Jill had never heard before. She could feel it in the ground under the soles of her feet. Even the children noticed it, and the four stood staring at each other while Jody whined, his tail between his legs.

Suddenly the dog's whining changed to a growl and, at the same time, Betsey let out a little scream. Jill wheeled about, the thought of rattlesnakes instantly in her mind. There was a clattering on the stones of the creek and three deer burst out of the willows, dashed past them and went leaping down the road. At almost the same moment a long, fog-gray shape appeared behind them, moving noiselessly but with amazing speed. It couldn't be. But it was! A mountain lion!

It's after the deer, Jill thought, but then she saw that it was carrying a cub by the nape of the neck as a cat carries a kitten. For the space of a heartbeat it paused, staring at them with fierce, yellow eyes. Then it swerved, passed so close that they could feel the stir of air behind it, and went bounding up the trail toward the old mine.

32

All at once a light seemed to explode in Jill's brain. Something she had heard or read about somewhere flashed into her consciousness. "There's been a cloudburst up above us!" she cried. "Quick, everyone! Up the trail! The creek's flooding!"

She grabbed Betsey's hand, herded the twins before her, and ran as fast as she could, with the roar now like cannonading in her ears.

4

Betsey was sobbing with fright as Jill half-dragged her up the steep path behind the scrambling twins. Jody ran ahead, but circled back from time to time to make sure that they were all following. The echoing roar now filled the whole canyon, punctuated by sounds like explosions. "What is it? What's the matter? I don't *want* to go up there where that old mountain lion went," Betsey wailed, struggling to hold back.

Jill had neither time nor breath to explain. All she could do was to lift Betsey bodily under one arm and climb on. Could they get out of reach of the flood in time? Would the water, like the noise it was making, fill the canyon to its brim and engulf them all? "Please!" Jill heard herself praying in a desperate whisper. "Please, oh please, God! *Please!*"

Once a stone turned under her foot and almost made her fall, but she caught her balance and struggled on. Still the appalling din continued to grow louder and louder. Suddenly before them, the wall of the cliff rose starkly perpendicular, and in it a boarded-up door that must be the old mine. They had reached the top: they could go no farther!

Fearfully, Jill turned and looked behind her, then continued to stare, frozen in helpless horror. For one short moment she saw the little glade just as before, dark hemlocks and willows and tall, rosy-trunked pines all dappled in sun and shadow. The stream, however, was running brimful and yellow with mud, the waterfall upstream was no longer white, and even while Jill's mind noted that fact she saw just above it a dark wall of water loom tower-high over the willows. For an instant it seemed to hang there. Then, with an even more savage roar, it advanced, and the tops of the willows disappeared under a crashing avalanche of foam-streaked brown that engulfed the glen, the cabin, the hemlocks, even the pines, as some enormous prehistoric monster might fall upon its prey.

Now they were staring down into a cauldron of swirling liquid, where brush, the trunks of broken trees, even rocks appeared briefly, tossed up above the surface, then disappeared below flat whirlpools and yellow spray. The pine under which they had planned to eat their lunch swayed wildly, fell with a crack like a gunshot, and was swept away. The chimney of the cabin caught and held it for a moment, then it whirled off downstream like everything else.

"Oh!" Betsey screamed. "There was a chipmunk there on that tree. I saw him. Oh, my poor little chipmunk!"

Jill had seen it, too, flattened desperately against the tree trunk. The sight brought into piercing focus the peril they all faced. How far up will the water come? Are we high enough to be out of its reach? she asked herself, but could find no answer. They were trapped, and they could only wait and see.

While the four watched, still paralyzed by its terrible fascination, the flood's dark, reptilian swirls and coils crept swiftly higher and higher up the trail. Now its spray was cold on their faces, and the shock brought Jill suddenly out of her numbed trance. She turned and looked again at the cliff. There was a small ledge only a few feet higher than where they stood, but even that might make the difference between life and death. She turned back to lift Betsey up upon it, but just then Sam gave an exclamation.

"Look!" he said. "It's not rising any more."

Yes, Jill saw, the height of the water was the same as when she had looked last, and even as she stared in disbelief it began to diminish. The noise, too, was lessening. "I think we're high enough," she said aloud, her voice a husky croak.

"It was a flash flood, like they tell about, wasn't it?" Peter said at last in an awed whisper.

No one spoke again for a long while as they watched the water slowly ebb away and lay bare its devastation. In that space, barely a quarter of an hour, the whole floor of the canyon had changed. The wide, shallow, clear-running stream had vanished and in its place lay a wild jumble of rocks, broken brush, prostrate, muddy willows, and uprooted trees. Where there had been carpets of green moss and pine needles there were now only ebbing pools of dirty water and swirls of sand, mud, and gravel. Even the waterfall above them was altered and barely recognizable.

"Look at our cabin!" Sam said, still whispering.

Jill stared. The cabin stood, but the entire structure had been moved from its foundations away from the fireplace and chimney, which now towered stark and alone like some ancient monument. The kitchen ell had been torn off and was nowhere to be seen.

"Our house!" Betsey cried. She turned and hid her face against Jill while sobs shook her whole small body. Jill knelt beside her and hugged her tight. "There, there, don't cry,"

37

she begged. "Houses can be built up again. We're all of us safe. That's what's important. Don't cry. Please don't cry!"

Jill herself was very close to tears. Gone was the lovely, fairy-tale glen, and what was left was hideous desolation. Abomination of desolation. The words came to her in a forlorn echo from somewhere in her memory.

"Golly, Jill, I guess we're lucky you knew enough to get us up here in time. I'll bet you saved our lives," Peter said. "And look, you brought our lunch along, too."

Jill looked down in amazement. Yes, there was the picnic basket beside her, although how she had managed to hold on to it she couldn't imagine.

Betsey stopped crying and peered inside it. "You spilled our milk though, Jill. Look, it's all over the sandwiches and cookies."

Abruptly, Jill began to laugh. She sat back on the ground weakly, unable to control her laughter, although she could feel tears starting in her eyes. I'm having hysterics, she thought, and fought for self-control. "Yes, I did spill the milk," she gasped. "Probably you think that Phoebe could have brought your lunch up here without spilling the milk, but I couldn't. All I could do was to get you three here ahead of the flood."

Three solemn, worried faces stared at her. Then Peter stepped forward and gave her arm an awkward pat. "It's okay about the milk, Jill," he assured her. "Golly, who cares about any old milk when we all nearly got drowned? Nobody could have got us up here faster than you did, that's for sure. Not even Phoebe."

"Did we nearly get drowned?" Betsey's eyes grew wide. "Did that truly happen to us? To me, too? Then this is a real adventure that we're having now, isn't it? Won't Mommy be surprised when we tell her about it?"

"Mom!" Peter turned suddenly stricken eyes to Jill, and

instinctively she looked at her watch. Had Mrs. Wendell still been in the canyon when the flood came? Jill felt her hands go wet and cold, her mouth dry. She tried to think of something to say, but nothing would come. It was plain to her that both boys were thinking the same thing, for their faces had begun to crumple. "Gosh, Mom!" Sam echoed.

Somehow Jill found her voice. "Your mother's all right," she declared. "She was going to Garrett's store, remember? The river doesn't come near it." She forced definite, cheerful assurance into her statement, and the twins seemed to believe her. But in her own mind there was no such conviction. The hands of her watch had told her a different story. There would not have been time for Mrs. Wendell to get to Garrett's store, and the narrow road between the high canyon walls would surely have been a deathtrap for any car in there when the torrent came down. The noise of the engine, echoing from the rocks, would have drowned out the roar that had alerted them, here. Horror rose within Jill like a sickness. Desperately, she pushed the picture out of her mind.

I must think about here and now, she told herself. Is the flood really over so quickly? How long must we stay here? Then another thought came to her and her heart gave another frightened plunge. The mountain lion!

The trail ended abruptly against the cliff, but just above them she saw fresh marks where the moss had been torn away. Was it done by great claws scrambling higher? Was the creature still up there on some ledge watching them, hidden by the overhang?

That decided her. "Let's go down a little way," she said quickly and herded them ahead of her again. Nor could she force herself to look back, even once, at the face of the cliff.

With awed and hesitant steps they went slowly down the path, then stopped, for the lower part of the trail had been washed away so that it ended in an abrupt drop, cut off as cleanly as though with a huge knife. As for the road by which they had driven into the canyon the day before, there was no trace to be seen of it—nor of the bridge which had spanned the lower waterfall. The other bridges would be gone too, Jill thought.

"There's the jeep!" Peter said. "I wonder where those men are?"

Wheels up, it lay half buried by sand and gravel and covered, too, by the branches of a sizable pine which had fallen across it. A vision of the station wagon in the same position flashed into Jill's mind and she drew in her breath, fighting down a dizziness that was close to nausea. She closed her eyes. Please, let this all be just a nightmare. Let me wake up in a moment and find that I'm in my own bed at home with my mother and father, Beth and Rick close by! But Betsey's hand still clung to hers and, when she opened her eyes again, the nightmare was still there.

"What'll we do? What'll we do now, Jill?" Peter asked. He and Sam were both looking at her, their eyes anxious, their mouths a little open.

Jill breathed in shakily. No, no, this mustn't happen to me, not to me, Jill Gray, she told herself. Not this. Because if— if Mrs. Wendell didn't get out of the canyon in time, if she—. Again the thought was too terrible to consider, and with all her strength she pushed it from the surface of her mind. But it *has* happened, and I'm left here in charge. Not Phoebe, but *me*. She clenched her cold hand on the handle of the basket. No matter how scared I am, I won't frighten these poor little kids, too, she vowed.

The three were still waiting for her to answer, but it was Betsey who broke the silence. "I'm hungry," she announced.

Then, with a great effort, Jill was able to find words. "Well, I guess the first thing to do is to have something to eat. After all, it's lunchtime," she heard herself saying, surprised by the steadiness of her voice. At least this was something to do. She turned to the basket.

"Peanut butter sandwiches and cookies all sogged up in milk! Who wants that?" Sam made a disgusted face.

Jill hesitated. Her mind seemed to have begun to function again. All our store of food was on the shelves of the kitchen ell, she was thinking, and where is it now? Maybe this, here in this basket, is all that we'll have to eat until help comes. Should we try to save what little's here until later, when we're really hungry? No, she reasoned swiftly. The milk-soaked sandwiches will turn sour and will be uneatable in a few hours.

Aloud she said, "Listen, everybody. This is all the lunch we have and we'd better not be fussy." She forced a grin. "Just pretend it's bread pudding and it'll taste delicious."

"Whoever ate bread pudding out of a basket, and with their fingers, too," Betsey said, giggling, and scooped out a handful. "Why, it's good!" she exclaimed and reached for more. The twins followed her example, but Jill, after a taste or two, abandoned the effort. Too many frightening questions were crowding into her mind.

Even if Mrs. Wendell were safe and sent help, with the road washed out wouldn't it be some time before anyone could get to them? If something *had* happened to her, what then? Reluctantly, Jill made herself face that possibility, also. Nobody below at the crossroads had seen them drive by. Nobody, not even her own family, knew exactly where they were, except Professor Wendell, and news of this flash flood in this remote canyon might not reach him at once. He might not even learn about it until he tried to join them on the weekend.

Soberly, Jill considered the problem. Should we make an attempt to hike out ourselves, she asked herself. Could we manage to follow down the steep-walled canyon without the road and the bridges? It would mean wading the stream, and in the narrow places it was a swift and dangerous cataract, perilous even for a strong, adult swimmer.

She looked up at the towering, almost vertical cliffs that shut them in. If we somehow managed to scale those rocks, what then? We'd have to make our way down the rugged, dry, chapparal-covered mountainside without a trail. There'd be the sun, she remembered, the terrible, deadly, midsummer sun, with no shade and no water.

No, it will be wiser to stay right here until Professor Wendell comes, she decided. At least we have shade and water here. But there would be other problems. Food, warmth, shelter, protection—things which Jill had always taken for granted now loomed before her as desperate needs that must be provided somehow, and by *her*.

Her eyes turned unwillingly to what had been, so short a time ago, a lovely, soft-colored little glen, and she felt a shiver move between her shoulder blades at what she saw there now. There lay the proof that in this mountain wilderness, which people used so gaily as a holiday playground, there were still ancient and mighty forces at work that must be reckoned with. Formidable, hostile powers that could easily swoop down and destroy without warning and without pity. Like the old pagan gods, she found herself thinking. No wonder the cavemen feared them so and sacrificed to them, trying to placate them all—the gods of flood and earthquake, ice and fire.

And *fire*! The words rang through her mind, and suddenly she almost laughed aloud in her relief, for an obvious solution had come to her. This may be ancient, unchanged wilderness, but these are modern times. Of course the thing to do is to build a fire! The sight of smoke will bring forest wardens at once, probably in a helicopter. We can find plenty of dry wood up above the floodline, she told herself. And there's the chimney and the fireplace still standing to build it in, thank goodness! Building a fire out in the open could prove fully as dangerous as the flood had been. She was about to call the twins, tell them of her plans, and set them to gathering wood when another thought stopped her. Matches!

She felt in the pockets of her shorts, but she knew, even as she did so, that it was useless. Nor would the boys have any, either, for it was a cardinal principle in the mountains to keep matches strictly away from children. Mrs. Wendell had reminded her of that only this morning. Could there be any left inside the cabin? Those she had used last night had been kept in a can in the kitchen, she remembered. But perhaps somewhere else—?

We'd better go down and look anyway, she thought. Just then Sam reached for an apple and Jill found herself putting out a restraining hand. "Wait. There may not be much else for supper," she told him. "They'll keep. Better save them for later."

"Okay," he said, cheerfully.

What nice, reasonable boys they are, Jill thought, with a rush of warmth. That's one thing I can be thankful for, surely. They're well-trained children, all of them. Aloud she said, "Well, shall we go down and have a look at the house?"

They scrambled and slid down the steep, muddy bank and made their way over the rubble to the cabin. The door was gone and other blank openings yawned where the fireplace and kitchen lean-to had been, but the walls and roof had held together somehow. Everything that had been movable inside had either been swept out and away or was now mixed with mud, sand, and gravel and piled in an indiscriminate mass against one wall. That's the wall where the clothes closet, the built-in cupboards, and the drawers are, Jill thought. No use in trying to get at anything there.

As for matches, the merest glance told her that there was no hope whatever of finding any here. A cold weight settled

43

in her chest, but after an appalled moment, she steadied herself and climbed inside, followed by the silent children and Jody. It seemed a miracle that the cabin had held together at all, but the bunks were still in place and the floor, although slippery with mud, seemed steady. As Jill stood looking about her, uncertain what to do next, the others moved closer to her, Betsey even pressed against her side, but no one spoke. The air seemed chilly, partly from the dampness and shadow inside the cabin but partly too, Jill realized, because the storm had cleared away the oppressive heat and left a definitely cool tang in the air. Noon had passed and Jill was familiar enough with the mountains to know that, with this change in the weather, evening would surely bring cold. The twins wore only their cotton shirts and jeans, and Betsey, like Jill herself, was in shorts and a sleeveless top. All their other clothing was in that closet or those drawers, blocked by a mountain of debris and undoubtedly soaked through.

Food, warmth, shelter, protection—the words raced through Jill's brain once again. The cabin, such as it was, would have to serve as shelter, although it could offer little else. From where she stood she could see that all the lower bunks were stripped of everything but mud and sand. But how about the two upper ones, where the twins usually slept? She crossed the muddy floor, climbed the ladder, and saw, with suddenly rising spirits, that their pads and blankets were still in place. What was even better, the pads were not wet, for the water somehow had not reached that high, while the blankets which covered them had received only some splashing.

"We might as well get these blankets out and dry them in the sun," Jill said. "And let's take down the curtains of the bunks, too," she added, for a new idea had come to her. The red curtains, spread out to dry, would surely attract attention from aircraft, if any passed over them. But I won't explain this to the children, she warned herself. It's better if they don't realize yet quite what a fix we're in. "There's a little warmth in the curtains, too, to use for bedding tonight, if we get them dry."

"Bedding?" Betsey exclaimed. "Are we going to sleep here again tonight? No, I don't want to, Jill. I want to go home just as soon as Mommy gets back. I don't like this cabin any more."

The twins had been very quiet during the whole proceeding. Now they turned to Jill, and she could read the frightened question in their faces. She hesitated, for it was all at once hard to get breath enough to speak. "That was a bad flood you know, Betsey," she said. "You saw that the road and the bridge here are gone. It probably washed out others, down below. Your mother may be delayed in getting back, and we should be prepared to sleep here tonight, if we have to."

"Oh," Betsey said. "Well, okay, but still I don't like this place any more at all. It isn't pretty like it was. It looks just awful and it's no fun. The woodpile's gone and my poor chipmunk, too."

A loud, frantic squawking now began somewhere outside, and at the same time Jody growled and the fur along his back bristled. "Well, there are your blue jays back again, anyway," Jill said, beginning to haul out the blankets.

"What's the matter with those old birds and with Jody, too?" Peter said, and he peered out of the doorway. Then, "Oh, Golly!" he exclaimed in a tone that brought Jill's heart into her throat.

"What is it?" she asked, climbing hurriedly down the ladder.

"I—I think it's that mountain lion again," Peter said, stammering a little in his excitement. "It was just disappearing and that's what the jays were yelling at. It went fast up over the rocks past the waterfall. Anyway, they were following something big."

"Oh boy!" Sam cried. "Let's see if it left any tracks."

Before Jill could protest, both twins were out the door and scanning the ground. "Yes, here's one, real plain," Peter cried in triumph.

Jill hurried to where he was crouched beside a patch of mud. The track was there, unmistakably large and clear and so fresh that it was slowly filling with water. How big it was, and how close it had come to them, again!

"My camera's somewhere in that mess. And I suppose it's wrecked, anyway," Peter mourned. "This would have been one swell chance to get a picture—in broad daylight, too!"

"Maybe it'll come back," Sam said. "Listen, Peter, did you notice if it was carrying its cub, like before?"

Peter wrinkled his brow. "I don't know. I really didn't see it very plain. It was gone so quick," he said.

"Well, if it wasn't, then it's left it behind somewhere up the old trail and it's coming back, sure enough."

"That's right!" Peter's face brightened. "Maybe there's a cave up there on the cliff above the trail. If we find it and the cub's in it we could catch it and tame it for a pet!"

"Oh yes, let's!" Betsey agreed, clapping her hands.

"Come on. We'll have a look," Sam said, and he was turning toward the trail when Jill caught him by the shoulder and whirled him about.

"Just a minute!" she said, and gave him a shake. "Wake up! You know better than that. What do you think the mother would do to you if she found you fooling with her cub?" She had begun to tremble, and it was all she could do to keep her voice from breaking. She was angry, too, but her anger wasn't so much against the boys' heedless rashness as against her own fright.

Sam looked sheepish. "Yes, I guess that's right. But it would sure be great if we could," he added with regret.

Jody had come with them and was sniffing at the tracks,

while the hair along his backbone bristled again and he growled low in his throat. He lifted his head and looked off in the direction in which the beast had gone, but he made no move to follow it.

At least he has some sense, even if he's only a puppy, Jill thought. He's just as scared as I am. Night's coming and we have no fire, no shelter or protection except that wrecked, waterlogged cabin without a door. She remembered all the night noises, the coyote's howls, the danger from rattlesnakes —where was their snake-bite kit now?—and this mountain lion. What other perils might be lurking in the great wilderness that surrounded and imprisoned them?

She brought herself up sharply and shook her head. There I go working myself into a panic. This isn't helping anything. I must *do* something so I won't have time to think and terrify myself and maybe them, too. "Come on," she said aloud. "We'll get the blankets outside and spread them over those fallen pine branches to dry, and the bunk curtains, too. And after that—" The idea came to her suddenly. "After that we'll go and see if we can find where our kitchen ell got washed to, because that's where our supper's gone."

5

All working together, they stretched the damp blankets and the red curtains in the sun over the branches of the uprooted pine. "It makes a nice sort of tent," Betsey said. "Why can't we sleep in there, Jill?"

"No, I think the house will give us better shelter from the wind," Jill told her. And it'll be safer than the ground from rattlesnakes, she thought, too, and suddenly resolved to use the upper rather than the lower bunks.

She looked up at the rectangle of bright sky. Surely any plane that passes over will notice all this bright red, she told herself. Then, even as she looked, something appeared, sliding silently across the blue. For an instant Jill thought it was a plane already and her heart gave an exultant leap. Then she realized that it was no plane but, instead, a huge, dark-winged bird, gliding on motionless, outspread wings—a buzzard—and the disappointment was like a blow.

Another then appeared, and the two shadows moved slowly,

one following the other as they made their great, sinister circles, while Jill watched them, chilled but still too fascinated to wrench her eyes away. Peter was watching, too. "Buzzards!" he said. "They're looking for dead animals to eat. I suppose there's a lot of them that the flood caught."

"Yes, I suppose so," Jill answered. His words had brought a terrible picture to her and she could barely hold the tremor out of her voice. "Well, let's go hunting for our kitchen," she added, quickly.

"Where do you guess it got washed to?" Sam asked.

"It would have been carried downstream, of course," Jill said. "Come on, let's look."

The four and Jody, too, picked their way down the rubble-strewn creek bed. Again Jill looked about at what she had thought of—so short a time before—as a fairy-tale glade. Now the sheer and towering cliffs and the ugly devastation all around had changed it into a rock-walled prison.

They searched through the confused flotsam of the stream bed and along its sides without finding anything but rocks, brush, splintered boards, and mud. Where the cliffs drew close together and the bridge had crossed the lower waterfall, however, the flood had evidently been dammed briefly before it broke through. The bridge was gone, of course, but larger beams and logs, shattered planks and timbers were scattered along the sides—some even hung caught in the muddy upper branches of the willows. How high the water had come, Jill thought, with a shudder. If we hadn't made it up the trail in time—!

"Those logs and boards are part of our house, sure enough," Sam said. "Look, there's our front door!"

"And there's our stove," Peter cried, pointing to where it lay partly buried in a great drift of gravel.

"A door and a stove," Betsey said. "But not anything for our supper."

50

Jill had been thinking the same thing as she scanned the scene before her. Somewhere in all this confusion, she reasoned, there must be some small part of the ample stores that had lined the kitchen shelves, but where? The packages would have floated and were probably miles away by this time, but surely heavier things, like cans, would have sunk when the force of the water was slowed down behind this temporary dam. They must still be here, buried in the mud and gravel.

As she stood considering the problem she recalled a day at the beach when Beth had lost a bracelet in the sand. Her father had divided the area where they had been sitting into definite sections. Slowly and carefully they had combed each one, inch by inch, sifting the sand through their fingers and then discarding it all on a single pile. That system might work here.

She explained her plan and the twins nodded. "Sounds okay to me," Peter said. "What'll we dig with?"

"With our hands—yes—and we can use sticks," Jill said. "You have your knives, boys. Go get us some good, strong sticks."

"It'll be a treasure hunt," Sam said. "A sure enough one, too, because I'd rather have something good for supper than golden treasure, right now."

"Or it's like the Swiss Family Robinson looking for salvage from their wrecked ship," Peter added, eagerly.

"Fine! Now get to work and cut us some diggers, you—you canyon castaways!" Jill said, and for the first time in what seemed to her like many hours she didn't have to force cheerfulness into her voice.

Finding suitable sticks and whittling points on their ends took some time. Meanwhile, Jill marked out an area on both sides of the stream behind the dam into sections. At last they were ready, and all set to work. Jody, seeing them digging, joined in, and the sand and mud flew behind his paws. He

51

soon tired, however, as did Betsey, but the twins worked persistently and after half an hour Peter gave a triumphant shout. "Here's something!" he cried. He held up a can. It glittered brightly in the sun, for the paper label was completely washed off. "What do you suppose is in it?" he asked.

Jill took the can and gave it a shake. There was no motion and no gurgle from inside, so it must be something fairly solid, she decided. "It's too big for soup. It might be roast-beef hash or even spaghetti—we had a lot of both of those," she ventured.

"Oh boy! I hope it's spaghetti!" Sam cried. "Open it quick, Jill."

Open it? With a suddenly sinking heart Jill stared at the can in her hands. They had no can opener, not even the old-fashioned, hand-operated kind! "Well, now we have another problem," she said, slowly, trying not to sound as dismayed as she felt. "Do you boys happen to have can openers on your jackknives?"

Solemnly they shook their heads. They even took out their knives to show her that neither one bore any such tool. "Just two blades, a big one and a little one," Sam said. "Can't we break the thing open with a rock?"

"No, that would only mash it," Jill said.

"Wouldn't one of our knife blades cut into it?" Peter asked.

"Maybe, if we hammered it with a stone," Jill answered. "But we'd probably break the knife, and it seems to me that your knives are pretty precious to us right now. I'd hate to risk it. We're going to get this thing open somehow, though, you can count on that. Just let me think. What else do you boys have?"

The twins emptied their pockets and laid the contents on a flat rock. Besides the knives, they produced a good deal of string, a small harmonica, a dried and twisted tube of paste, several paper clips, a ball of tin foil, and four odd marbles.

Jill's own pockets contained nothing but a red cotton bandanna and a small comb.

"Mom made us put on clean pants yesterday before we started," Sam said. "We just haven't had time to accumulate much." He dug deeper into a pocket. "Well, here's some nails."

"A nail!" Jill cried. "That just might do the trick."

She chose the largest of them, set the can on the rock, and using a stone for a hammer, began to pound a line of holes around its rim. She punched the holes as close together as she could so that they would meet each other and so make a continuous cut. It was a long and tedious process, for the nail kept slipping. Once she pounded her finger and the pain was so sharp that tears rose to her eyes, but she shook her head impatiently and kept on. At last, by cautiously using a knife blade to pry with, she was able to make a wide enough opening to see what was inside.

"Dog food!" Sam exclaimed. The smell had already given Jill some warning, but the words were nevertheless bitterly disappointing to hear.

"Dog food!" Peter echoed. "Golly! After all that work!"

"Well, Jody has to have something to eat for supper, too," Betsey told them brightly.

It was an effort for Jill to hold back the sharp answer that was on her tongue. She sat on her heels sucking at her pounded finger and wishing with all her heart that she could let loose the tears of frustration that were so close to the surface. Her arms ached and there were blisters on both her palms from the rough digging stick. Worse than the pain, however was an inexorably logical conviction that was filling her mind. If that's the only food we can find we mustn't waste it on Jody, she was thinking, yet the idea of feeding that disagreeable-smelling mess to the children or of eating it herself nauseated her, hungry though she was.

Four apples and a can of dog food! She bit down on her lip. Tired or not, we simply have to keep on searching. We're not going to give up now. She got to her feet and picked up her stick again. "We found one can, and that means we're looking in the right place," she said, aloud. "Back to the treasure hunt, my merry men! And we ought to keep hunting where Peter was digging. There may be more there."

"More dog food?" Sam snorted. "Not me. I'm digging somewhere else."

They all worked on, pausing to rest from time to time, while shadows slowly gathered and lengthened and a cool wind began to blow through the canyon. At last, Jill saw something shining in the mud and unearthed it eagerly. It was another can, larger than the first, and it gurgled when she shook it. Opened by the same slow, laborious method, it proved to contain stewed tomatoes. "That's an improvement, anyway," Jill said.

At almost the same time, Sam, who was still digging at a little distance, gave a whoop and held up a flat, rectangular tin. "Sardines!" he shouted. "And the key's still stuck on it, too. Talk about luck! I think all cans should be made like this. Maybe we could get somebody to pass a law about it."

"But *you* don't like sardines, Sam. You never eat them," Betsey reminded him.

"I'm going to eat these, you betcha, and like them, too," her brother told her.

They dug, with more and more frequent pauses, for the rest of the afternoon and found three more cans of various sizes. "Why don't you open these, Jill?" Peter asked.

Jill shook her head. "Once they're opened they won't keep," she said. "We have enough food for tonight, so we'll save these in case we need them tomorrow. Besides, the sun's going to set pretty soon, and we'd better bring in our bedding before the dew falls."

Tired, wet, muddy, yet somehow triumphant, they carried their treasure-trove back to the cabin. They ate the stewed tomatoes from the plastic cups that were in the picnic basket and the sardines with their fingers. It was an odd and very messy meal, but no one complained. Jody openly enjoyed his dog food and lapped up the oil from the sardine can when they had finished with it. The twins had brought in the blankets and the red curtains, and Jill made up the two top bunks, for the lower ones were still wet and muddy.

"Two of us can sleep in each bunk, you boys in one, Betsey and I in the other," Jill said.

"Two in a bunk. That'll be awfully crowded," Sam objected.

"Yes, but we'll use the same covers and keep each other warm, too," Jill explained. "It's getting cold now—you can feel it—and it'll be a lot colder tonight. We'll have to sleep in our clothes, too, of course."

"I guess you're right," Peter said. He paused, eying Jill with an odd, shy look. "You're really pretty good at figuring things out for us, Jill," he said, and there was such sincere admiration in his freckled and very dirty face that Jill felt suddenly absurdly proud and well-rewarded.

"No toothbrushes and no bathroom and no pajamas!" Betsey said. "However can we get ready for bed, Jill?"

"We really need baths, all of us," Jill said. "It would probably make us feel better to get clean, but I guess we'll have to skip them until morning. The creek's still too muddy, and besides, it's cold and there's no way of getting warm afterwards. We're awfully dirty, though, aren't we? Let's see. We haven't any soap or any towels, but here's my bandanna. We can use that for a washcloth and it'll be dry by morning."

They found one pool where the water had settled enough to be fairly clear and Jill washed all the faces in turn, then her own. She combed out Betsey's tangled curls with her pocket comb, thankful for the twins' crew cuts that didn't need to be combed. All the while, she kept up a running stream of cheerful talk, for she could sense that evening and dusk were bringing uneasiness to the three children. "I just know that Mommy misses us," Betsey said at last, when Jill had finished with her hair. "When will they get the road fixed, Jill?"

"Well—" Jill began, but Peter interrupted.

"I'm real worried about Mom, Jill," he said. "You know, that water came awfully fast. If she *was* in the canyon—"

"We must all put special thoughts for her in our good-night prayers," Jill told him, quickly. It was the only thing she could think of, and, to her surprise, it seemed to help. She even found herself making up a little prayer of her own as she boosted Betsey into her bunk and tucked her in.

"No television and no radio," Sam said.

"No books or magazines or games or puzzles or anything, either," Peter added. "No place to sit, even, except the wet floor or that big pile of junk—and it's wet, too. It's too early to go to bed, but there's nothing else to do, so I guess we might as well." The twins then climbed into their bunk where, after a good deal of shifting and some argument, they settled down at last.

Betsey was already asleep when Jill clambered cautiously in beside her. Jody watched the proceedings from the floor, picked out a fairly dry spot, turned round and round many times in the age-old manner of dogs, then curled up with every indication of comfort. It would be wonderful to get to sleep as easily as children and dogs, Jill thought. Now that she was lying still she found that her back, as well as her arms, ached from the digging, the blisters on her hands stung, while her finger kept up its painful throbbing.

Then the night noises began and, open as the house now was to all outdoors, they were louder than ever. The rush of

56

the waterfalls, the insects, the tree frogs, the night birds, the many obscure and mysterious rustlings, all seemed to be right in the cabin with them. The coyotes' yipping, too, no longer came from far in the distance. If I didn't know better, I'd think some of those beasts were just outside that open door, Jill thought, lying rigid in the bunk to listen.

There was another noise, too, that came faintly at long intervals—different from anything she had heard before—strange, eerie—almost like a human shout. Was it perhaps the mountain lion prowling somewhere, stalking its prey through the shadows, its great yellow eyes like lamps, as she had seen them so briefly but so unforgettably?

If only we had a fire or some sort of weapon or even a flashlight, Jill thought. There are the digging sticks, but they're down there on the floor. I'd better get them and keep them up here with me. I could at least throw one at anything that came inside, she decided, although clambering down into the darkness took some resolution.

Jody stirred and whimpered as she passed him and Jill paused. Wouldn't the little dog be tempting prey for coyote or lion? She placed the digging sticks in her bunk, then climbed down and lifted Jody into it, too. "There you are. You'll be safe here," she whispered, giving him a pat. He wagged his tail and licked her hand, then settled down at the foot of the bed.

The darkness seemed to be growing less dense inside the cabin and soon a patch of moonlight began to slide in barely perceptible motion along the floor. The chill increased, for a wind had risen. Jill could hear it in the few pines that were left standing. It's almost like the noise the waves make below us on the beach, she thought, and got some comfort from it, for she so often listened to the surf from her own bed at home.

The twins were sleeping soundly and so was Betsey. As

the cold increased, however, Betsey began to cough and her small, compact body kept burrowing closer and closer into Jill. Jody, too, was restless, and whenever Jill shifted her position to make herself more comfortable he would begin to whine in his sleep while his paws made frantic running motions against her legs.

He's having nightmares, Jill thought. I wonder what he's scared of? At least *he* doesn't have to act brave and wise and set a good example. Oh, if only Phoebe were here instead of me! This is the sort of situation she could handle. I'm as likely as not to do something stupid and make a fatal—a *really* fatal —mistake! If someone should be bitten by a rattler, for instance!"

She turned restlessly, forgetting for the moment the other occupants of the bunk, and Betsey sat up. "Mommy!" she wailed aloud.

Jill gathered her close in her arms. "It's all right, darling," she murmured, rocking her back and forth as she could remember her own mother doing, long ago. "It's all right. Go to sleep."

Tears were in Jill's own eyes. They spilled over and she could feel them running down her cheeks. The dreadful conviction that had haunted her all day long since the flood, that she had tried not to let herself think about, now rushed upon her with overwhelming force. Surely, if by some miracle Mrs. Wendell had escaped the flood, she would have sent help for her children. Even though the road was gone, a forestry helicopter could have made it and it would have reached them before this.

No, the station wagon was lying somewhere down the canyon, wrecked and overturned and buried in the mud like the jeep. And the driver? The mother of this little girl, of those two fine, sturdy little boys—? It's wrong! It's not *fair!*

Jill told herself and she was filled with a hot anger that seemed suddenly to dry her tears.

She laid the now sleeping Betsey down again and tucked the covers around her. Her mind had begun to work with new calmness and clarity. Today's Tuesday, she thought. Does Professor Wendell usually come up here on Friday or on Saturday for the weekend? I'll find that out from the boys in the morning. Even if it's not until Saturday, that means only three and a half days, at the most. I can manage until then.

What was it that Phoebe said to me there in the cafeteria that day at the beginning of the year? "You have as good a brain as mine, Jill. You could do anything—and I mean anything—if you wanted to hard enough."

Well, this is the time when I find out whether or not that's true. Because I know that never before and never again in all my life will I want anything so hard as I want to keep these three poor little kids safe. *And I'm going to do it.*

6

Jill must have fallen asleep after that, because the next she knew the sun was shining and Jody was moving restlessly about in the bunk, looking down at the floor and whining.

"All right, I'll get you down," Jill told him. "Ouch!" she exclaimed an instant later, for when she started to sit up a sharp twinge caught her in the small of her back. Her exertions of the day before had left her muscles so stiff and sore that every movement was painful. She was climbing slowly and carefully down the ladder with Jody under one arm when her ears caught a sound that held her in a sudden frozen paralysis. Was it another flood? For one agonized moment she listened, clinging to the rounds of the ladder. Then, recognizing the noise, she dropped Jody and jumped the rest of the way down. A plane! A helicopter!

She ran out the door, aches and pains forgotten, only to see the craft just disappearing from her sight down the canyon. "Wait!" she called. "Wait! Come back! We're here. Oh, *please* come back!" Although she knew it was useless, she kept on running and waving after it, stumbling over the rough ground until something tripped her and she fell to her hands and knees. Tears started in her eyes, but she rubbed them angrily away with both fists. That was a forest ranger helicopter looking over the damage that the flood made, she told herself in helpless fury. If only I had left our red curtains out, they'd have seen them, as I planned. How could I have been so stupid as not to have thought of that? And—oh, dear—they couldn't even have noticed the jeep, either, it's so covered up by that tree! I wonder if they'll come back. I'll get the curtains out right away again, on that chance.

The twins and Betsey were still fast asleep when Jill pulled the red cloth off the boys' bunk and carried it out into the sun. She was spreading it on the big sand bar in the middle of the stream bed when Peter appeared, yawning, in the doorway. "What're you doing, Jill?" he called.

"Come and help me," she answered. "Get all the big, light-colored stones you can find. A helicopter just flew over, and I'm going to spell out a message on top of this red cloth in case it comes back again."

"What sort of message?" he asked as he joined her.

"Why, 'help,' I guess," she said.

"No, let's make it 'S.O.S.,'" Peter urged. "That'll look more important."

"Okay, but come along and do it. Call Sam, too, while you're about it," Jill told him.

Sam appeared and the two boys joined in the work. "I know where there's lots of real white stones—or used to be before the flood," Sam said. "Up there past the willows. Come on, Pete, let's go get those."

The boys disappeared, but in a moment both of them were back, wide-eyed and pale. "Jill!" Peter said in a faltering, breathless voice. "There's a dead man up there, Jill."

62

Jill straightened up from her work and stared at him, but her mind refused to accept what she had heard. "A what, Peter?"

"A dead man—drowned, I guess," Peter insisted. "He's lying there on the bank all muddy, his clothes torn."

"I think he's one of the men in the jeep," Sam said. "Anyway he's got sneakers on—or one sneaker, at least. Come on and see for yourself, Jill."

Reluctantly, with a pounding heart, Jill followed the twins. There, beyond the willows, like a heap of muddy clothes, lay a figure that was still unmistakably human. Jill paused, her mouth dry and cold, unable to go any nearer, but Jody, who had followed them, went close, sniffed, then began to bark.

Abruptly, the figure gave a sort of groan and sat up. Gray eyes stared at them from a mud-streaked face. "Hello," he said.

"Hello," Jill answered automatically, while relief flooded through her in a warm, reviving tide. "You're *alive!*" she added, in wonder.

Through the coating of dried mud that covered him even to his hair, Jill could see that the man was young, after all, perhaps no more than Rick's age, and that his face had crinkled into a grin. "Yes, I guess I am, at that," he said. "But only just. Boy, am I glad to see you! But say, how about my friend, Dr. Curry? Have you seen him? Is he all right?"

Jill shook her head. "No, we haven't seen anybody else," she answered. "But your jeep's there, what's left of it."

His face darkened. "I thought the jeep would be gone. But I was still hoping Dr. Curry had made it, somehow."

"What were you doing in our canyon, anyway?" Sam asked.

"We were collecting specimens," the boy answered. "We had back-packed up from where we left the jeep and we'd made camp beside the water a few miles upstream. We hadn't any warning whatever of the flood, nothing but some rolls of thunder. It didn't rain on us at all. I was fairly high up on the side of a cliff when the water came, but Dr. Curry—he was right down there in the bottom. He's sort of deaf, too, and he didn't even hear me when I yelled to him, nor the noise of the flood either, I suppose. The water caught me and knocked me around some, but I managed to catch hold of a tree and climb into it. I didn't see him at all, though, after that first minute." His voice cracked a little and he stopped speaking, while the others stood looking at him in helpless sympathy. "I sure hope he managed to make it, somehow," he added, at last.

"Did the flood carry you all the way down here?" Peter asked in awe, after a pause.

"No," the boy told him. "I hung on in the tree, as I said. Then, when the flood had passed, I climbed down, and that's when I found out that something had happened to my ankle. I guess it's sprained. I couldn't walk on it, so I kind of crawled along, following the canyon and hollering every once in a while to try to locate Dr. Curry. I kept on all afternoon and into the night, until I got tired and lay down here and went to sleep. Gosh, I didn't realize I was this close to civilization!"

So that was the sound I kept hearing in the night, Jill thought, the sound that had seemed more human than a puma's cry.

The boy was looking at them expectantly, and now the meaning of his last sentence came suddenly to Jill. This close to civilization! Of course, he thinks he's reached safety at last, whereas—. Well, I'll have to tell him how far wrong he is, she was thinking, when he spoke again. "Say, could you call someone—your dad, maybe—to help me along? I can't walk, you see."

"Our dad's not here, nor our mom, either," Sam told him. "We're canyon castaways."

"Castaways?" the boy echoed.

"What Sam means is that when the flood came we were

here alone and it's washed out the road. Nobody's been able to get back since then. So we've been calling ourselves 'castaways' like on a desert island," Jill explained.

"Alone? Just you three little kids?" the boy exclaimed.

"We're *not* little kids!" Peter corrected him. "Jill's fifteen and we're ten. There's our sister, Betsey, though. She's little. She's only five years old," he added.

The boy smiled briefly, then his brows drew together again. "Say, that's real tough. Was that your house, that cabin in the little glen? Is it washed away, too?"

"It got sort of knocked around, but it's still standing," Jill told him. "About your ankle, though. Does it hurt a lot?"

"Not too much, except when I try to move it," the boy answered. "Well, I guess I'll have to keep on crawling for a while."

"Wait. Maybe if I bandage it up it'll feel better," Jill said. "I've taken first aid. I could do a pretty good job."

"What'll you use for bandage?" Sam, always practical, asked.

"Why—I can cut a piece from one of the curtains, of course," Jill answered. "Let me have your knife, Sam. Just wait here—. My goodness, I don't even know your name! Mine's Jill Gray, and this is Peter Wendell and this is Sam."

"My name's Greg, Greg Murdoch," the boy told her. "How do you do?" he added.

"How do you do?" Jill answered, stepping forward and holding out her hand. Greg grasped it and they shook hands gravely. His palm felt cold and gritty to Jill. How chilly he must be after a night in the open, and he's in pain, too, she thought. "Wait here," she told him as brightly as she could. "I'll be back in a jiffy and fix you up."

One of the curtains is smaller and shorter than the others, she remembered as she ran into the cabin. I'll use that one for the bandage. As she entered Betsey coughed, turned over, then sat up, sleepy-eyed, in her bunk. "Hello, Jill. I'm hungry," she announced.

That's another problem, Jill thought. *Another mouth to feed,* as they said in the old stories. But of course we'll have to manage. She pulled the shorter red curtain off the bed and cut through the selvages with Sam's knife, then tore a sizable square from it. I do remember how we bandaged ankles, thank goodness, she told herself, though I never did it on anyone with an actual sprain. The main thing is to make it firm enough to hold the joint rigid, but not too tight.

"What are you doing, Jill?" Betsey asked, peering down at her. "Mommy won't like it a bit to have you tear that curtain. And I want my breakfast."

Jill explained about their visitor, whereupon Betsey scrambled down the ladder and hurried out to see him for herself, breakfast forgotten for the moment.

When Jill returned she found Greg sitting with the children in a small circle around him. Peter jumped up at sight of her. "What do you think Greg was collecting?" he asked, his eyes round and shining. "Ants!"

"Ants?" Jill repeated, smiling. "Of course he's kidding."

"No, that's right," Greg told her. "Dr. Curry's on the staff of the Museum and he's an authority on ants. We were out on a hunt for a very rare kind that's been rumored to be in these mountains. We found some, too." His face darkened. "I had some good specimens in a little container in my pocket, but of course it's gone. That pocket got caught on a snag and ripped off. I had my little microscope in it, too. A good one," he added.

"What a shame!" Jill said. "Well, shall I start with my first aid?"

"Okay," he said, and thrust his foot gingerly forward.

Jill could tell how painful the motion was, for his face paled suddenly under its grime, and tiny drops of sweat

66

gleamed on his forehead. She knelt down and, as gently as she could, drew off the wet sock. The ankle was swollen and purplish blue, with streaks of red.

"Golly!" Peter exclaimed. "That looks awful! Maybe it's blood-poisoned."

"If it is, it'll have to be amp— amp— cut off!" Sam said. "Did you learn how to cut off people's feet in first aid, Jill?"

"Don't be silly!" Jill told him. "It's only a sprain, that's plain enough." She herself was none too sure, for she had never seen a sprain before in all her life, and the color and swelling were alarming. This was no time to reveal ignorance, however. Tongue between her teeth in concentration, she set to work, infinitely thankful for the fact that, because she had failed her first test in the bandaging of a sprained ankle, she had had to repeat it and practice it over and over again. Now the steps of the process returned clearly to her. She folded the square into a triangle and set to work.

At last it was done and tied in place, with the corners of the bandage neatly tucked in. "There!" she said, and sat back on her heels. "How does it feel, Greg? Is it too tight? It mustn't be, you know, but it still ought to be firm enough to keep the joint from moving."

"Feels great," he told her, moving his leg cautiously. "You're a pretty good doctor. Thanks a lot."

"Now suppose you boys look around and find a strong stick for Greg to use for a cane," Jill said. "Then we'll all help him up on his feet and get him down to our cabin."

"Yes, and then have our breakfast," Betsey said. "What do you suppose it will be?"

"Gosh, I hope it's spaghetti this time," Sam said. "Anyway, not dog food!"

Greg looked puzzled and Jill tried to explain. "We salvaged some cans from the flood but the labels are all washed off, so we can't tell what's inside until we open them," she said. "By the way, do you happen to have a knife with a can opener on it?" she asked with sudden hope.

Greg shook his head. "My knife's gone. It *did* have a can opener on it, and also something to get stones out of horses' hoofs," he added, with a brief grin. "But it's gone, anyway. How *do* you get your cans open?"

"With a rock and a nail," Jill told him. Then—she almost knew it was a useless question, but still she must ask it. "How about matches?"

He shook his head again. "I did have some in a waterproof container, as all woodsmen should, but they went with the other things. Wait a minute, though!" His fingers searched the pocket of his shirt and brought out a wet and pulpy something that might be—that *was* a book of paper matches!

Jill's heart gave a great leap. We can dry them out, of course we can! This sun's hot enough to dry anything. We'll dry them and build a fire and that will be the end of our troubles here. The fire wardens will come like a shot the moment they see smoke rising. She was about to explain this to Greg—how nobody knew of their plight, her fears for Mrs. Wendell's fate—everything—when she remembered about the children and caught the words back. The twins were off hunting for a stick, but Betsey was close by. "That's wonderful," she said, aloud. "We'll dry them in the sun and then we can have a fire." I'll tell him the whole situation later when the kids aren't around, she decided. Not now.

The boys returned proudly with a stick that was not only strong and the right length but which also had a wide-angled fork on the end that would make a good crutch. By all four boosting and pulling together they got Greg to his feet—or rather to one foot, where he balanced precariously for a moment as he fitted the new crutch under his arm. Erect, he was much taller and broader than Jill had realized. Then,

68

with the help of the crutch and with the twins on either side to steady him, he hopped his way down the bank of the stream to where the cabin stood.

"It did get sort of knocked around, for sure!" he said, looking at the skewed-about structure. "Is all that out there your laundry?" he added, at the sight of the red curtains stretched on the sand bar.

"That's our signal to the airplanes, if any more come over," Peter explained. "So far there's been mostly buzzards, but we're going to mark out S.O.S. with white stones. The S.O.S. was *my* idea, but the rest was Jill's. She's our baby-sitter—or at least Betsey's—and she heard the flood coming and knew what it was and got us up that trail, there, in time. I guess she saved our lives."

"And she saved our lunch, too, but it was only wet pudding," Betsey finished.

Over the two red heads and the curly yellow one, Jill's eyes met Greg's. His were crinkled again with amusement and she grinned back. He's *nice*! she thought. I wonder what he looks like when he's clean? Suddenly she looked down at herself. Her own clothes were almost as grimy as his, from her digging the day before. She hadn't so much as combed her hair this morning, and her face was probably dirty, too.

"How about breakfast?" Peter asked. "Shall I bring out one of the cans, Jill? Which one?"

"Whichever looks the least like dog food," Sam said, and hurried after him.

"All our food got lost in the flood when our kitchen was broken off the house," Betsey explained to Greg. "We went digging for cans yesterday, like for buried treasure, and the first can we found had dog food in it. None of us people wanted any, but it was nice for Jody, all the same."

"You mean you haven't any fire or any food left either?"

Greg asked, looking suddenly grave. "Say, this isn't the best time to have company drop in on you, is it?"

"Don't say that!" Jill told him. Her eyes suddenly filled. "I'm so glad you're here!" she added, and there was a small tremor in her voice.

"Jill's kind of a scaredy-cat," Betsey felt called upon to explain once again. "She's afraid of rattlesnakes—and mountain lions, too."

"Seems to me that Jill's been doing okay, scaredy-cat or not, and you're mighty lucky to have her along," Greg said, with such sudden, almost fatherly, severity that Betsey's eyes grew round. She put her thumb in her mouth and said no more.

Peter now returned carrying a large can. "It doesn't gurgle," he said, shaking it as he came. "What do you suppose it is?"

"Let's everyone guess, and the one who's right gets the first helping," Jill suggested.

"I guess spaghetti!" Sam shouted quickly.

"Roast-beef hash!" Peter cried.

Betsey thought for a long time and finally suggested corn flakes. When this was hooted down by the boys, she was given another chance because of her age. "Well then, oatmeal," she countered, and would not be swerved from that choice.

"It's pretty big. Maybe it's canned peaches," Greg ventured. "They'd surely taste good for breakfast."

"We told you it didn't gurgle, but you've used up your turn, anyway," Sam said. "How about you, Jill?"

"I think it might be sweet potatoes," she said. "I saw some cans of those on the shelves and this seems about their size."

"I think they'd gurgle too, a little," Peter said. "There's always some sort of juice in the bottom. Open it, Jill. Let's see what it is."

Jill set the can on the flat rock and produced the carefully hoarded nail from the pocket of her shorts. "Wait—I can do that much for you, even if I am a cripple," Greg said, taking the implements from her.

"You boys finish getting the white rocks and spell out the S.O.S., then," Jill said. "I'll set the table, if we can call it that."

"I'll stay here and keep Greg company," Betsey offered. She seated herself as close as possible to Greg, looked up into his face from under her lashes, and smiled. "I like you," she told him. "Do you like me?"

"I like all *good* little girls," he answered in a gruff voice, whereat she giggled and snuggled closer. "*I'm* good," she assured him.

Over her head, Greg winked solemnly at Jill, then turned to his job. Jill went back to the cabin and brought out the basket containing the plastic pitcher, which she filled with fresh water from the creek. She brought the cups out, too, and also one of the empty cans to use for a cup. It's too jagged for the children, but I can manage with it, she told herself.

The sun was warm by this time and the stream had begun to run clear at last. Birds were singing in the muddy, bedraggled willows and in the other trees that had remained standing. Jill's spirits lifted. Greg's arrival had brought amazing comfort to her, she discovered. She no longer felt alone, solely responsible for the safety of the children. Crippled though he was, he was *there*. And he had brought matches, too, she remembered suddenly. I must get them out in the sun so they'll be drying.

The twins had now gathered a sizable pile of white stones, but they were arguing about something. "Well, let's make the 'O' in the middle first, then," Sam said. "It can only go one way. Hey, Jill, how does an 'S' go?"

Jill traced the outline in the air for him, but when she went to look at their work a moment later the 'S' was backward. "I did it just like you showed me!" Sam insisted.

71

"I was facing you, remember?" Jill said. "I should have thought of that, myself."

"Maybe from the air it'll look frontward," Peter suggested.

"No it won't," Sam scoffed. "You're thinking about in a mirror."

They rebuilt the 'S,' made a large round 'O' in the middle, then another 'S,' and stood back to see how it looked. Peter even climbed a little way up the side of the canyon to make sure and came down pleased. "It looks swell from up there," he reported.

Jill then laid the paper of matches carefully in the middle of the 'O', where it would be in the full sunshine. I hope getting so wet hasn't spoiled them altogether, she thought anxiously. She made sure not to touch either the matchheads or the strip where they were to be struck as she bent them this way and that, separating them so that the sun could reach each one.

"Well, I've got the can open. None of us guessed right," Greg called from his seat on the flat rock.

"What is it?" The twins shouted the question as they raced toward him.

"Come and see. I'm not too sure," Greg answered.

"It's some sort of yellow goo and it smells terrible," Betsey added.

Jill peered into the opened tin. "Canned squash!" she said, after an appalled moment.

"Canned squash!" Sam echoed. "Gosh, I think I'd as soon have dog food!"

"Let's try another can," urged Peter. "Can't we, Jill?"

Jill hesitated. They had two more cans still unopened. Moreover, the matches would certainly be dried in a few hours. They could then build their fire, the smoke would bring the forest rangers, and all their food problems, at least, would be solved. She was about to yield to the twins' appeal when, from overhead, came a rush of wings and a loud squawk. Before their horrified eyes, a blue jay swooped down into the middle of their red signal, snatched up the paper of matches in his beak, and flew off over the treetops.

7

"Our matches!" Betsey screamed. "Oh, that horrid, mean old bird! After all the crumbs I fed him, too!"

"Our chance of a nice campfire!" Sam said.

"I was going to catch some fish and we could have cooked them," Peter mourned. "I was planning on how I could make fishhooks out of those paper clips."

And the chance of alerting the fire wardens and bringing them to our rescue, Jill thought, but she bit down on her lip and held the words in. Greg didn't say anything, so, after a long moment, Jill answered Peter's question. "Squash is nourishing food and there's lots of it in this can," she stated. "It will make a good meal for all of us. We certainly aren't going to waste it, now that it's open."

The twins still looked rebellious. "I don't see why we have to eat that icky goo when there're other cans that might have something good in them," Sam protested. "Mom'll send someone to get us out real soon, road or no road, you can bet on that. Why, they might even come in a helicopter and give us a ride! It's not as if we were going to have to stay here much longer."

"The trouble is, we don't know *how* much longer, Sam," Jill told him. How could she convince them of their plight without revealing the horror of her fears for Mrs. Wendell? After a moment, an idea came to her. "You see, maybe the reason why your mother hasn't sent help is that she's been trapped, just the way we are, by the washed-out road and the high canyon walls."

This was a new and hopeful thought for Jill herself, and it brought a small sense of relief to her. She was able to speak more cheerfully as she continued. "Remember, nobody down at the crossroads or the ranger station knows that we're here. We didn't stop at the store, and Mr. Garrett was asleep and didn't see us go by. We may even have to wait here for help until your father comes this weekend. He'll get us all out then, never fear. What day does he usually arrive, Friday or Saturday?"

"Friday," Sam answered. "He mostly comes Friday evening in time for supper."

"This is only Wednesday morning. That means three whole days that we ought to plan for. Until we get hold of more cans or something else to eat we'd better—"

"Wait!" Peter spoke suddenly. "Don't you remember, Sam? Dad wasn't coming at all this weekend. He was going to a convention or something, up in San Francisco."

"That's right. Gosh, I'd forgotten all about it," Sam nodded.

Jill could only stare at them. Again there was silence, except for the rush of the waterfalls and a bird's distant piping. At last, Greg shifted his position on the rock. "Well, I reckon that means squash for breakfast for all of us," he said. "And listen, you kids. Any sure-enough castaways on a desert island or in a canyon, either, would think canned squash was a real

76

treat. So would those tough old pioneers crossing the plains, or the mountain men, the 'long rifles,' either. Citified fuss-budgets wouldn't have lasted very long with them. They had to eat lots worse things, you can bet on that."

"And so did polar explorers, too. I was reading a book about them," Peter agreed, catching the idea eagerly. "It'll sure taste better than tallow candles, like they had to eat. Or their own boots, either. I've always wondered how they managed those!" He looked down in doubtful speculation at his sneakers.

"Boiled them and made them into stew," Greg told him. "But we haven't any fire, remember, so boots are out for us. It'll have to be the squash."

"And everybody who finishes his share of squash can have a slice of apple for dessert," Jill promised.

Betsey peered into the can. "However can we eat it without any spoons? We can't even drink it out of our cups, the way we did with the tomatoes. Shall we use our hands?" And she poked a grimy forefinger toward the thick, yellow purée.

Jill moved the can out of her reach. "Wait. Boys, can't you whittle us out some spoons? We might as well eat as decently as we can manage."

The spoons proved to be more like small paddles, but they served their purpose. Jill dished out carefully measured shares into the four plastic cups for the children and Greg, leaving what was left in the can for herself. Then Jody pushed close to her, looking up with such pleading brown eyes that she spooned some of hers out on a flat stone for him, too. At first he only sniffed at it, then, surprising them all, licked it up and wagged his tail for more.

"A very sensible pooch, that," Greg said. "He'd have done well crossing the plains or in the Arctic. Nothing sissy about *him!*"

This praise for Jody spurred Betsey and the boys to follow his example. With no further protest, if without enthusiasm, they silently downed their portions. It doesn't taste good at all, but it must be filling, at least, Jill told herself as she swallowed her last mouthful. She had read somewhere, too, that yellow vegetables were full of vitamins, and that should help.

When they had finished and each had had a slice of apple, Sam stood up. "I guess you and me'd better go downstream and dig for more cans, Peter," he said. With no prompting from Jill, they shouldered their digging sticks and set off, sober and purposeful. Betsey then curled up again beside Greg while Jill took the spoons, the cups, and also the empty can down to the creek to wash them.

The news that Professor Wendell wouldn't be coming at all this weekend had shaken her, and even now as she worked, she hardly dared to face what it meant for all of them. She was still a little hungry, too, for she had given much of her share of the squash to Jody. I suppose that wasn't very bright of me, she thought, but I couldn't resist his eyes. What if we can't find any more cans, though? We probably won't starve to death in a week and a half, but we'll certainly be awfully hungry. And what—what if something happens to delay Professor Wendell?

Only the fact that Greg was here to share her responsibility helped to ease the fears that loomed within her. At least I'm not alone any more. He seems to know a lot about the woods, and he understands how to manage children, too.

"Do you have any younger brothers and sisters, Greg?" she asked him when she returned to where he still sat with Betsey.

He grinned. "I'm the oldest of six," he told her.

"Oh!" Jill exclaimed. "That must be wonderful—for them!"

"Well, I don't know about that. I rule 'em with a rod of iron, but they seem to like it. They're all good kids. These are, too," he added.

"Especially me," said Betsey. "I'm good *almost* all the time."

"I'll wait and make up my own mind about that, young

lady," Greg said, but with a wink that took the severity out of his words.

Betsey giggled, then gave a squeal and jumped up, clapping her hands. "There's my chipmunk!" she cried. "He came back. He didn't get drowned after all, Jill."

Jill hadn't the heart to tell her that all chipmunks looked much alike and that this was probably another one. "That's fine!" she answered, instead, and the little girl raced away after the frisky-tailed creature, with Jody frolicking behind her.

Now's my chance to tell Greg how matters really stand—about my fears for Mrs. Wendell and all, Jill thought. Quickly she poured out the story to him. "I'm really awfully scared for her. I haven't said that to the children, of course, but according to my watch she must have been right in the steepest, narrowest gorge when all that water came down. Do you think she could possibly have survived?"

"It looks grim," he said. "About Dr. Curry, too. I *saw* the water sweep him under. All that force! It was tossing rocks around like soap bubbles. Nobody could have lived through it. He was a nice old guy and mighty good to me."

"Mrs. Wendell was nice, too," Jill said. Oh dear, I didn't always think so, she remembered, and now that memory seemed wicked and heartless. Her throat filled. "And when I think of these poor little children—!"

"Yes, it's the youngsters we've got to plan for," Greg said, after a little pause. "Have you thought of trying to hike out with them?"

"Yes, I did, right at first," Jill answered. "But then when I saw how the road here and this first bridge were gone, I knew that the rest of it would surely be washed away and all the other bridges, too. We'd have to wade the stream and it's far too swift in the narrows for the children—or anyone else, for that matter."

79

"That's for sure," he agreed.

"We might try to climb out of the canyon. Maybe we could, from farther up the stream. But that would make the trip a lot longer and over really rough country. Away from the creek, the mountainside is practically desert. There would be no shade, just that tangled chapparal, and the sun's awfully hot. This is June, almost July, remember. I don't believe we could make it. Betsey's so little—."

"Desert sun isn't anything to fool with at any age," Greg said, nodding again. "If I hadn't busted up my ankle like this, I might make it and send help back, but it would take too long, hopping and crawling. Yes, the best bet is to stay here. At least we'll have water and shade. Besides, that red cloth and your S.O.S. may catch some airman's eye soon."

"If we could only build a fire!" Jill said, after another pause. "Smoke would bring fire wardens to us right away. That's why losing those matches seemed so awful."

"I doubt if they'd have lit, anyway, after getting so wet," Greg said.

Jill was wondering if that was true or if he had said it only to make her feel better, when they heard Jody begin a frantic barking and, an instant later terrified screams from Betsey.

The *mountain lion*, Jill thought, jumping to her feet. I never should have let her go off alone. She ran as fast as her feet could carry her toward the sound, leaving Greg to hobble after as best he could.

There was no sign of any mountain lion, however, as she came in sight of the two, and Jill felt an instant of relief. Betsey stood with her hands over her face, still screaming, while Jody danced back and forth, barking at something just under the branches of a fallen tree. Then Jill saw what it was and her heart seemed to stop within her. It was a rattlesnake, coiled and ready to strike, it's tail a blur while the high, menacing buzz of its rattling filled the whole world!

But there was Betsey within its reach! Jill snatched the little girl up and whirled her a safe distance away. "Did he strike you? Are you hurt? Did he bite you?" she cried.

"No, but he *wants* to!" Betsey wailed, clinging to her. "Don't let him, Jill. Please don't let him."

"I won't, darling, I won't," Jill told her and in her relief she squeezed her so hard that Betsey gasped for breath.

"Not Jody, either," Betsey sobbed, as soon as she could get the words out. "Don't let him bite Jody either, Jill."

Jill looked at the little dog still so valiantly holding the enemy at bay. "No, I won't. I won't let him get hurt, either," she promised, wondering in wild desperation how she could halt what looked like an inevitable tragedy. Greg was hobbling toward them—Jill could hear his crutch on the stones—but he was still too far away to help. A big rock caught her eye. Quickly she pushed Betsey aside, caught up the rock, balanced it for a moment to aim it, then flung it as hard as she could into the middle of the coils.

Knocked out of its striking position, the snake seemed momentarily stunned, and at that moment Greg arrived. He leaped forward on his good foot and caught the rattler just behind its head in the fork of his crutch. "Hit him with the rock again, on the head!" he shouted.

The twins had arrived by this time, and Peter seized Jody by the collar and dragged him away. Sam seemed to hesitate, daunted by the savage buzzing and wriggling, so Jill picked up the rock once more and smashed it down again and again on the ugly flat head until there was nothing left of it but a shapeless something in the dust. Then she turned, walked a few unsteady steps, felt her knees buckle under her and sat down. I guess maybe I'm fainting, she thought in astonishment. What was it that we learned to do for fainting in first aid? She couldn't remember and slumped forward.

The next she knew something cold was dripping onto her face. She opened her eyes to see a ring of anxious visages staring down at her. "I'm all right," she said, struggling to sit up, then sinking back again weakly. "Truly I am. Don't look so scared. Is the snake really dead?" she added, trying to keep the tremor out of her voice.

"He's still wriggling. We can't be sure if he's really dead until sundown," Peter said. "They don't die until the sun sets, you know."

"Huh! Who believes that old story!" Sam scoffed. "It's not true, is it, Greg?"

"I'm sure this snake is plenty dead enough, thanks to Jill," Greg assured him.

"Thanks to you, really," Jill said, and closed her eyes against the picture that had leaped into her mind. "And Jody, too. Where is Jody?" she asked, sitting up to look around.

"He's over there, trying to eat up the snake," Betsey answered, pointing. "Won't it give him a terrible stomach-ache, Greg?"

Greg hobbled quickly over to where Jody was worrying at the still squirming reptile. "Give me your knife, one of you," he ordered. "I've got to get the head off and bury it. Then we can let Jody eat all he wants to. The head and fangs are still dangerous even after the critter's dead as a doornail."

"Are you real sure eating it won't make Jody sick?" Peter asked.

"Rattlesnake meat is very good," Greg stated. "If we had a fire we'd sure cook it and eat it ourselves. I've had it and liked it."

The mere thought of that was enough to turn Jill faint again, but she swallowed hard and changed the subject. "Did you boys have any luck?"

They shook their heads. "Not yet," Sam said.

"But I've just thought of something," Peter added. "There used to be a patch of wild strawberries growing on a ledge across the creek. We got some there last year, remember, Sam?"

"Wonderful!" Jill cried. "Take the basket and get any that are ripe. But take your sticks along and—and watch out for rattlers!"

"We sure will," Sam promised.

And mountain lions, too, Jill almost called after them as they trotted away, but managed to hold the words back. She got to her feet. Her knees were still a little shaky, but her voice was steady enough to sound natural when she spoke again. "You certainly got here fast, Greg," she said, when the boys were gone. "How's your ankle feeling? Is the bandage still firm enough?"

"It's fine," he said as he hobbled back toward his flat rock. On the way he stopped beside one of the pools left by the flood. "I'd sure like a wash, though."

"We used to take shower baths in that waterfall," Betsey said. "It was lots of fun."

"Why don't you try it, Greg?" Jill suggested. "That is, if you can manage it without hurting your ankle. Betsey and I'll go into the cabin and stay there so you needn't try to be modest about it. When you're through, just call out."

"Fine!" he agreed. "But I'll have to put these muddy clothes on, afterwards."

"No—I'll go and bring out a blanket for you," Jill said. "You can wrap yourself up in it while I rinse out your clothes. Betsey and I'll hang them in the sun. They'll be dry in a jiffy."

When Greg's shout summoned them from the cabin, they found him bundled like an Indian chief in the camping blanket. "Those clothes of mine are pretty awful," he said. "I hate to have you bother with them, Jill."

"It's no bother, but I may not be able to get them very clean with cold water and no soap," Jill said. "At least I can rinse the sand and gravel out of them."

"You look different," Betsey said, walking around Greg to inspect him from all sides. "Lots better. Being clean does help a person's looks, doesn't it?"

Jill was thinking the same thing. His rugged, blunt-featured face was deeply tanned in contrast to his gray eyes, and she could see now that his hair was a nice medium brown. He's certainly not handsome, like Rod Campbell, but he looks husky and—and dependable, she found herself deciding as she gathered up his clothing.

The clothes were dismayingly dirty, and Jill had never washed anything by hand in her life except her own under-things. How in the world did one go about it, she wondered. Somewhere she had seen travel pictures of peasant women in foreign lands washing clothes at a river's edge, rubbing them and beating them on flat rocks. Since I've no soap, that might be the way to manage it, she decided, knelt down beside the water, and set to work. And while I'm about it I could wash my own face and comb my hair, too, she added, catching a revealing image of herself reflected in the pool.

As she worked there in the cool, running water, Jill was conscious of a new and pleasant sensation—a feeling of well-being, almost of exhilaration. I suppose it's because of the danger that we just barely escaped, she thought. No, it's more than that. I was so scared of the snake—scareder than I've ever been before, probably—and afterwards I fainted like a ninny, too. But that was *afterwards*. I did grab Betsey out of the way and I did hit the awful thing with the rock when I had to.

It's been an awful feeling, all my life, to know that I'm

84

not smart or brave, but being afraid of *acting* like a coward has been even worse. This one time when it really mattered I did what had to be done. I didn't act like a coward until after the danger was over. Maybe next time there's danger I won't even be afraid!

8

Jill and Betsey draped Greg's clothes carefully over the fallen tree branches. The sun was so hot that by the time they had the last of them in place the first were beginning to stiffen. "It won't be long—you'll have your clean laundry in time to dress for dinner," Jill announced. "Service is pretty good at this resort."

"Better than the meals, if you ask me," Greg answered, grinning.

Betsey pointed an accusing finger at him. "Now who's being a fuss-budget?" she demanded.

"You're absolutely right, Miss Robinson Crusoe, Junior," he answered. "Well, here come the berry pickers. Any luck?"

Both the twins were so stained around the mouth that the question seemed unnecessary. Proudly, they displayed almost a pint of berries in the basket. "We tasted some to make sure that they were okay," Sam explained. "And there's more there, too, that will be ripe soon."

"Oh, can we eat them now, Jill? Please?" Betsey begged. "I'll get our cups so you can divide them for us." She didn't wait for an answer, but ran off at once toward the cabin.

"Is that okay, Jill?" Peter asked anxiously.

Jill hesitated only a moment. "Why, yes. If there's more where these came from we can eat what you have here now. After all, they're pretty ripe and they won't keep," she answered, thankful that for this once she didn't have to be the frugal hoarder.

When Betsey returned Jill began to portion out the berries, counting them one by one into the plastic cups and the extra can. "At least we don't have to share *these* with Jody," Sam said. "Look at him. He's so full of snake that he can hardly waddle."

Jody, visibly sated, had rejoined the group, but after a scornful sniff in the direction of the berries, he turned away and stretched his length in a shady spot.

"Wait!" Peter said suddenly. His face was sober and a little red and it was obvious that the words were costing him something. "Me and Sam *did* eat quite a lot, up there in the berry patch, so don't give us such a big share as the rest, Jill."

"But gosh! we picked them, didn't we? Why shouldn't—?" Sam began, then stopped.

Troubled, uncertain what she should do, Jill looked from one to the other of the boys. This is important, she thought. Peter's done something really special in making that offer, and I mustn't spoil it. "Why, that's very honorable of you, Peter," she said, finally. "We do have to share everything carefully now, don't we?"

She then proceeded with the dividing of the berries, skipping the twins' cup on every other round. "There we are. Fruit for a midmorning snack, as it says in all the health books. And with the compliments of the Wendell Brothers."

When the last juicy morsel was gone, Jill turned again to

88

the twins. "Those were really wonderful and just what we all needed. Thanks a lot, both of you. Now how about fixing a place for Greg to sleep tonight? Will you clean the sand and gravel out of one of the lower bunks for him? You can use that big squash tin for a scoop. While you're doing that, I'll go and try my luck at digging for cans. I think there's still one section we haven't explored, yet."

"I'll stay here and keep Greg company," Betsey offered. "Someone ought to, and me and him are very best friends."

"*He* and *I*, Betsey," Jill corrected, automatically.

"No, not you, Jill. *Me* and him," Betsey insisted. "He likes me the very best of everyone. Don't you, Greg?"

"I like all good little girls. I told you that before," Greg answered, smiling across at Jill. She, to her embarrassment, had felt her cheeks grow warm and she hurried off downstream with her digging stick.

The feast of delicious berries had satisfied Jill's hunger for the moment. After only a few minutes of digging she uncovered a can that was obviously sardines and another large, cylindrical one. She could find no more, however, and as the morning drew toward noon the sun became so hot and the blisters on her hands so sore that she gave up the search.

When she returned with her two prizes she found that the boys had not only cleared the bunk but had discovered the corner of a blanket sticking out of the pile of debris against the wall. Several heavy rocks had held it down, but Greg, now in his dry if wrinkled clothes, had come to their aid. Using sticks for levers, they had moved the rocks and extricated the blanket and were now spreading it in the sun. "It's full of sand, but when it dries we can shake most of that out," Peter explained. "Now Greg'll have a bunk *and* a blanket."

"Room, board, and laundry, all for free," Greg said. "Guess I'll stay a while."

Everyone laughed as though this were the wittiest remark in the world, and the laughter echoed back to them from the canyon walls. Jill laughed with the rest, but as the echoes faded she saw a shadow come sliding along the ground. It passed over their little group, bringing an instant of chill. Jill looked up. There were the buzzards once more, circling darkly against the vivid blue. Realization of why they were there stabbed through her. How can we joke and laugh when maybe Mrs. Wendell, somewhere down the canyon—? And Dr. Curry, too!

Greg had seen the buzzards, but he made no comment. "Say, Jill," he said, sticking his bandaged foot out. "I got this wet in the shower and it seems to have shrunk. Could you loosen it a bit for me?"

"Of course," she said. "I'll get another one to put on while this one dries."

She brought another square from the cabin and untied the wet bandage as carefully as she could. She could tell how painful the process was, nevertheless, by the sudden stiffening of Greg's jaw. At the sight of the ankle, still so swollen and discolored, Peter gave an exclamation. "Say, that looks worse than before. Lots redder."

"That's dye from the bandage, most of it," Greg said, peering down. "It isn't pretty though, is it?"

"I never knew people's skin could be so many colors all at once," Betsey said. "There's blue and purple and red and even some places that look green."

"Green! That *must* be gangrene!" Sam cried. "Honestly, Jill, that's real dangerous. I'll bet it ought to come off."

"Sam Wendell, you stop saying such stupid, wicked things!" Jill said, surprised even as she spoke by the hot explosion of fury within her. "You don't know a thing about it, so just—just hush up!"

"Okay, but—but—!" Sam said. He stared at Jill as though

a firecracker had suddenly gone off in his face. "Gosh!" he repeated.

Jill bent to her rebandaging, already ashamed of her outburst. I blew up like that because I'm not a bit sure, myself, that I'm doing the right thing, she thought. What if Greg's lamed for life because I've bungled something? The idea was almost too dreadful to consider.

It was Betsey who broke the uncomfortable silence. "I'm awfully hot," she said. "I want to have a shower in the waterfall like Greg did. Jill, you make the boys stay inside the house so we girls can have a turn at it."

"All right," Jill said, tying the ends of the bandage and tucking them under. "And afterwards the twins can have a bath, too. It'll make us all feel better. Maybe I won't be so crabby then, Sam," she added.

His round, still troubled face cleared. "Oh, that's okay. Forget it," he told her, beaming once more.

The running water felt wonderful to Jill, after her hot and grimy morning of digging. Betsey squealed with delight as she hopped in and out under the waterfall or rolled about in the smooth basin that it had worn for itself over the years. Even after the twins began to shout impatiently from where they were cooped up inside the cabin, Betsey refused to emerge, and Jill had, at last, to lift her out by force. She managed it with difficulty, for Betsey's small, wet body was as slippery as a frog's. She kicked and resisted all the while, although her lips had turned blue and her teeth were chattering aloud.

Now, too late, Jill recalled what Mrs. Wendell had told her before she drove away. The words came back accusingly. "Betsey chills easily. She still has a cough left over from a bad siege of bronchitis last winter."

I should have remembered, Jill told herself, while frightening visions of fever and pneumonia raced through her mind.

She rubbed Betsey down with the rough blanket until her skin fairly glowed, but even after she was thoroughly dry and dressed, Jill could see her shiver from time to time.

"What's for lunch?" Peter demanded as the boys rejoined them at last after their showers.

"Bring out the smallest of the three round cans that are left," Jill said. "If it isn't something that's nourishing, we can use the sardines, too."

They all gathered to watch while Greg pounded the nail holes and opened the can. As before, Sam guessed spaghetti and Peter roast-beef hash. "I think it might be soup," Jill ventured.

"Baked beans, that's my guess," Greg said, whereupon Betsey nodded. "I guess baked beans, too. I'm on Greg's side," she stated.

"Horray!" It *is* spaghetti!" Sam yelled, when the can was opened far enough to see. "Spaghetti with cheese and tomato. That's my favorite. Whoopee!"

"This'll be a sure-enough feast," Greg agreed. "And we won't need to open the sardines, after all. Cheese is protein, too, and we may not be so lucky with the next can. How about it, Jill?"

She nodded with some reluctance. "I guess that's right," she said, trying not to sound as disappointed as she felt. The cold shower had whetted her appetite, and the can really wasn't very large.

By this time, to Jill's relief, Betsey had stopped shivering and seemed her normal self. The spaghetti, even cold, was delicious—and it was filling, too. When Jill returned from washing out their cups and spoons she found Betsey curled up, fast asleep, beside Greg, and she brought out a blanket and tucked it around her.

"What'll we do now, Jill?" Peter asked. "I don't think there are any more cans there at all."

"I've been wondering about what's still inside the cabin, in the drawers and cupboards and the closet, behind that pile of stuff," Jill said. "Perhaps we ought to start to dig that out. It'll be a hard job, but we might find something useful— even a supply of matches. I know that our clothes are in the closet and in some of the drawers. They'll be wet, but we can dry them and they'd be a change and help us to keep warm at night, too."

"That's a good idea," Greg said. "I can work at that. I can dig stuff loose and the boys can carry it out and dump it."

"Maybe we can find my camera," Peter said.

"Soaking wet and full of sand! What good would that be?" Sam asked scornfully.

"Wait a minute!" Peter said, suddenly greatly excited. "Mom brought a box of chocolate bars, remember, Sam? She keeps them on hand for treats, you know. She used to put them on the kitchen shelf but—well—some of them kept disappearing." He grinned sheepishly. "So last year she began hiding them. They're probably in one of those cupboards."

"That's right. I remember seeing her taking them out of the car," Sam cried. "Oh boy, let's get at it!"

With only their hands, their sticks, and the tin cans to dig with, the work went slowly. Greg loosened the mass of rubble while the others shoved it out the door. They unearthed a chair, first of all, with one leg missing, several waterlogged pillows and some pulpy bundles that had been magazines. "They were on the table," Jill said, remembering. "Isn't it strange that they are here and the table itself is gone?"

"Floods do queer things," Greg said. "There doesn't seem to be much logic to them."

Jill paused in her work to look out the doorway to where Betsey still lay asleep on the rock. She seemed very small and defenseless from this distance, and very much alone. I shouldn't have left her there all by herself, Jill thought with sudden dismay. That mountain lion!

The little girl stirred sleepily but didn't waken as Jill gathered her up, blanket and all, and brought her inside the cabin. As Jill laid her in a bunk she noticed that Betsey's cheeks looked redder than usual. She touched one with a tentative finger. It felt startlingly hot. Is she feverish? No, surely a fever couldn't start so quickly, Jill told herself, but uneasiness rose within her. Added to the danger from hunger and cold and wild beasts, was there now a threat of illness?

Soberly, she turned back to where the boys had paused from their labors. "Betsey sure sleeps hard," Peter said, chuckling. "Sometimes Mom gets her up and has to walk her around to make her wake up. It's real funny to watch."

A little relieved by this information, Jill set to work again. By now the debris was cleared away from in front of one of the upper cupboards. "Well, I guess we can get into this one," Greg said. "What's kept in there?"

"That usually has Dad and Mom's stuff in it—playing cards, writing paper, pens, and things," Sam said, climbing onto the pile to reach the handle. He tugged at it but the cupboard door refused to budge. "It's stuck," he said.

"Warped by the water," Greg said. He himself then climbed up clumsily, with the help of his crutch, and jerked hard at the handle. It came off in his hand—so suddenly that he almost fell over backward. "Well, that's that!" he said in disgust as he regained his balance. "But if there's only those things in it, we'd better start on another. Where do you keep your camera, Peter?"

"No special place. Mom put it away when we got here, in one of those cupboards or drawers, but I don't know which one," Peter answered.

"That's sure one thing we don't need," Sam said. "A camera, and especially one that's soaking wet. What I hope we find is that chocolate!"

Greg said nothing but set to digging again, and the others followed suit. They dug out another chair, a whole one, this time, and paused long enough to sit in it, each one in turn. "Chairs are a real good idea, aren't they?" Sam said. "I wonder who invented them? I bet he made a million dollars!"

"Chairs were invented long before dollars were, dummy!" Peter told him. "It was some caveman, probably. He got tired of sitting around on rocks and figured out a chair. Maybe they elected him chief, just for that."

"Or maybe they chose him king. Perhaps that was when thrones began," Jill suggested.

"More likely just *chair*man of the committee," Greg added.

They were all laughing at this mild sally, when Betsey gave a sudden deep, hoarse cough and sat up in the bunk, her cheeks crimson. "I don't feel very well!" she wailed between spasms of coughing. "I—I think I'm going to throw up!"

9

Jill sprang across the room. She had been scooping out sand with the big squash tin and it was still in her hand. She reached Betsey with it just in time. "One of you boys run and get the pitcher full of fresh water," she called over her shoulder as she mopped at the coughing, sputtering child with the first thing she could grab—her own bandanna. "There, Betsey, there! You feel better now, don't you? You'll be all right in just a jiffy. Don't cry, darling."

"I feel terrible!" Betsey sobbed as soon as she could speak. "I don't like it here any more. I want my own room and my own bed to be sick in, and I want my Mommy, too!" She pushed Jill away with both hands, hands that were so hot that their touch almost burned. "I want my Mommy!"

The twins had returned with the water, and Jill began to bathe Betsey's face and hands gently. "We'll get you home to your own room and your own bed, Betsey. Don't worry about that. We'll get you home the very first minute we can, the absolutely very first minute," she assured her.

Betsey's sobs eased, she drew a few more shaking breaths and looked up at Jill through wet, star-pointed lashes. "Is that a promise, Jill? A truly promise? Where's Greg? Will he promise, too?"

Greg hobbled close and bent over her. "Here I am, honey. Yes, I sure do promise, an honest-to-goodness, cross-my-heart promise," he said, smiling down at her. He reached out a brown hand and patted Betsey's flushed cheek. As he felt its heat his glance met Jill's. She saw his smile fade, but almost at once he forced a grin again. "Now, since that's settled, Betsey, you listen to what old Doc Greg has to say. Just you lie back and take a good nap. That's the treatment she needs now, Nurse."

"Okay, then, if *you* say so, Greg," Betsey said and closed her eyes obediently.

Jill waited beside her until her breathing became regular. The twins, now sober and subdued, tiptoed over and looked down at their sleeping sister. "I guess she's real sick, isn't she?" Peter asked. "She's probably got a fever, too. She has them with her bronchitis. That's what she gets all the time, bronchitis."

"Mom has some medicine for her in a bottle somewhere," Sam said. "It was probably on the kitchen shelf along with the snake kit and the other first-aid things, though."

Again Jill and Greg exchanged concerned glances. "Are you sure it was on the kitchen shelf, Sam?" Jill asked, after a moment's frowning thought. "I don't seem to remember seeing it when your mother showed me the snake-bite kit."

"Well, no, I'm not real sure," Sam said, hesitating. "Wait a minute! I remember, now. She had it in her hand that first afternoon along with the box of chocolate bars, didn't she, Peter? And she hid those somewhere in here, in those cupboards. I'm sure about that. She made us wait outside while she hid them, but I could hear her opening and shutting some door."

Peter nodded. "Yes, that's right. You see, that medicine's real sweet and Betsey likes it a lot. This spring Mom caught her trying to take some by herself, so I guess she decided she'd have to hide it along with the candy."

Jill drew a long breath. "If it's there we'll find it!" she said. "That's the most important thing for us to do right now."

"And finding the box of chocolate bars is the second most important thing, isn't it? Gosh! Wouldn't a bar taste good this minute!" Sam exclaimed.

Nobody disputed this, and they all set at the job again. It was slow, hard work with the poor tools they had, but at last another of the three upper cupboard doors was cleared. Greg clambered up, tugged gingerly at the handle, and this time the door opened, to everyone's great relief. The contents proved disappointing, however. No medicine, no chocolate bars, not even the camera. Nothing but old magazines left over from last year, packages of crayons, most of them broken, two pairs of blunt-pointed scissors, a flat tin box of water colors, a jar of rather dried-up paste, some jigsaw puzzles, and a stack of colored construction paper.

"Nothing but stuff for kindergarten kids!" Sam said in disgust. "Nothing we can use at all!"

"Those things'll be good to amuse Betsey with if she's going to be sick for very long," Peter offered, but without enthusiasm.

The cabin was filling with afternoon shadow when they finally cleared away the debris from in front of the last of the three upper cupboards. That door stuck, at first, but after a few attempts, Greg was able to get it open. "Blankets!" Jill exclaimed. "At least those are things we can use. It'll be cold tonight again, too."

They were only thin cotton sheet blankets, but they were

99

new and there were six of them, enough for everyone and to spare. "This means we won't need the red curtains for warmth, tonight. We can leave them out to serve for a signal if any plane should come over real early tomorrow, the way that helicopter did today," Jill added. "That reminds me. We ought to bring in the blanket we were drying out for Greg, before the dew falls. Will you bring it in, boys? Be sure to shake as much sand out of it as you can."

"Okay," Sam said. "I wish those blankets had been the box of chocolate bars, though. Or even Betsey's medicine," he added, quickly.

"Let me have one of your knives before you go," Greg asked. "I've been thinking it'd be a good idea to try to open that first cupboard door, the one that's stuck, before we dig away any more of the pile we need to stand on."

Peter handed him his knife and the twins hurried out, plainly glad to be relieved of the tedious chore of hauling out rocks, sand, and gravel. As soon as they were gone, Jill turned anxiously to Greg. "Betsey has an awfully high fever, I *know* she has! It came on so suddenly, too, Greg. It scares me."

"Yes, she's pretty hot, but then, kids do run up fevers fast," Greg said. "I remember times when one of my kid brothers or sisters seemed to be burning up, but they got over it all right. My mother just hauled out the old croup kettle. Boy, I can smell that thing still—." He broke off, his face grave, graver than Jill remembered seeing it. For a moment the two faced each other in the silent room. "That's right, don't say it. We haven't any croup kettle—or any way to heat it if we had one," he finished, his voice grim.

As though to make things worse, Betsey stirred, turned over, and began to cough, and it seemed to Jill that her cough sounded far deeper and hoarser than ever before. Still coughing, Betsey sat up. "I'm thirsty," she croaked.

Jill hurried to her with a cup of water. Betsey drank it down eagerly and asked for more. "When will we go home?" she asked. "I wish I was home right now."

"Soon, darling, just as soon as ever we can," Jill promised. "You'll have to have a good nap first, though. Won't she, Greg?"

"That's right," Greg told her. "It's a long trip, remember, and you'll have to be rested and fresh as a daisy before we can start."

Betsey looked from one to the other with round, doubtful eyes. "Well, okay," she said, at last. Then, as she had before, she lay back in the bunk and squeezed her lids tight shut.

When she seemed to be asleep at last, Jill spoke again. "Oh Greg, this is *my* fault! I shouldn't have let her stay under that cold waterfall so long. Mrs. Wendell warned me not to let her play in the brook because of the bronchitis she had last winter, and I forgot all about it! It'll be *my* fault if she—." Her voice choked and she couldn't go on.

"Take it easy, there. You've had plenty on your mind these last two days—no wonder you forgot one thing," Greg said, with gruff reassurance. "And for Pete's sake don't cry about it!"

"I'm *not* crying!" Jill protested, rubbing the backs of her wrists across her eyes. "Goodness, that wouldn't help anything, would it? It's just that I do hate to have been so stupid when I've tried so hard to do everything right, the way Phoebe would have."

"You're not stupid. For one thing, remember that if you hadn't really been on the beam when that flood came down Betsey wouldn't have had even this chance to be sick! Keep that in mind and stop stewing over what's past and can't be helped. And let's forget about that Phoebe character, too. The thing for us to do now is to find Betsey's medicine before it gets too dark to work. My guess is that it's in that stuck cupboard. High up in there would be the logical place to put something out of reach of kids."

"Do you think you can whittle a hole in the door? Is that why you got the jackknife?" Jill asked, feeling now greatly heartened by his words and also by his plan for immediate action.

"That's right," Greg answered. With the help of his crutch, he climbed up on the pile of debris to where he could reach the cupboard door. "If I can't do it this way, I can probably break it in with a rock. But if I try that, it'd be just my luck to smash the medicine bottle, too. I'll work at this first and see how it goes."

"I can spell you off when you get tired," Jill offered. "It must be hard to work balancing on one foot."

Greg only grunted in reply. It *was* hard work, she could see. The wood of the cupboard door was evidently tough, and for a while he seemed to make little impression on it. Betsey sat up, roused by the sound of his labors. "What's Greg doing?" she asked.

"He's trying to get the cupboard open so he can find your medicine," Jill answered.

"Good! I like that medicine," Betsey said. "Is that where Mommy put it? I was wondering."

"Greg thinks so," Jill told her. "But the door's stuck and it'll take him a while to open it. You might as well go to sleep for a while."

"I like that medicine," Betsey repeated. Her eyes were very bright in her flushed face and her voice had a hurried, breathless sound. "And I like Greg and I like *you*," she added. "I like Greg the very best of all my friends, and next best—" she hesitated. "Yes, the next best I like you. I like you better even than Phoebe. She's sometimes sort of bossy, and when she sings her voice hasn't such a nice sound as yours does, even if she does know all the words. Sing me something now, Jill. Sing 'Frog Went A-Courtin'.'"

Kneeling beside the bunk, Jill began very softly to sing the old tune. "I can't hear you," Betsey complained, moving her head restlessly. "Sing louder, Jill."

Jill had purposely kept her voice low. Despite Betsey's praise, she was none too sure of her singing ability, and Greg's presence made her doubly shy about it. There was no help for it now, however, and she launched more loudly into the second verse. To her surprise, Greg began to join in with a whistled accompaniment while he worked, adding a few trills and flourishes at the end of each stanza. Betsey seemed to doze off before they had finished the song, but by that time Jill was enjoying their duet so much, herself, that she kept on to the very end.

"Say, we're pretty good at that, aren't we?" Greg said when it was over. "Maybe we ought to put our act on the stage. Let's try another one."

"Sing 'Betsey's Boat's the Silver Moon,'" Betsey murmured sleepily. "That's my very own song, made up just for me. It's my special good-night song with Daddy. He sings it for me every night when he comes to tuck me in."

Jill smiled at the little girl's claim on the familiar old song, but at the same time she felt her eyelids sting, and there was a huskiness in her voice when she began. It soon cleared, and a moment later Greg's whistle joined in with soft, flutelike notes that wove in and out around the melody. Jill could remember only the first verse, but when she hesitated at the end, Betsey opened her eyes and whispered. "Go on, don't stop. Sing it over again. Sing it lots of times."

It was Greg who finally broke off—with an exclamation. "There! The hole's big enough. I can get my hand inside."

Jill jumped to her feet and Betsey sat up in the bunk, wide awake again. Greg snapped the knife shut, put it into

103

his one good pocket, and reached through the opening he had carved in the cupboard door. There was a long moment of silence while he groped about inside. "There're several different sized boxes. Some of them seem to be packs of cards," he said. "Wait! Here's something else. It's a bottle, all right, and it feels sticky, the way cough mixture usually does. Boy, I hope—!" He drew his arm out carefully and held his find up to the light. It was a bottle almost full of red liquid. "Let's see what the label says: 'Betsey Wendell. One teaspoonful in half a glass of water four times a day for cough,'" he read aloud.

"That's my medicine!" Betsey cried, clapping her hands. "Give me some of it right away, Greg. It tastes real good, just like the raspberry syrup we sometimes have on pancakes."

"Well, Nurse, here's the treatment for our patient," Greg said, handing the bottle down to Jill. "You'll have to guess at what's a teaspoonful, but it probably doesn't have to be too accurate."

Jill hurried to get a cup and fill it half-full of water, then carefully measured into it what seemed to her close to a dose of the red medicine. The world seemed suddenly golden to her, all the brighter now for the dark depths of woe in which she had been foundering such a short time before. It's because of Greg, she thought. He knows all about little children because he has so many brothers and sisters. He's really completely marvelous, besides, and so *nice*. He likes my singing, too. Maybe—maybe—I wonder—? All kinds of possibilities flashed through her mind. Couldn't this perhaps be the beginning of something truly special? After all, what could be more romantic than to meet one's true love during a dangerous adventure like this? It could almost be the plot of a movie!

Betsey swallowed her dose, licked her lips thoroughly, and smiled like a small angel. "There, now!" she said. "*Now* I'm going to have a good nap—just see if I don't. Good night, sweet dreams, everybody!" She lay back, turned over on her stomach and almost instantly fell asleep.

Instead of coming down from the pile of sand and gravel, Greg had turned again to whittling at the hole. "I felt a lot of different sized boxes in there," he said. "Might as well find out what they are. I thought I could pull the door open now that I can get a grip on it, but it's still tight. I'll have to enlarge the hole to get the rest of the things out. Peter's camera might be in there, you know."

"His camera?" Jill repeated in surprise. "What do you want with that? I thought you were looking for the chocolate bars."

"Those of course, too," he nodded. "But if I can find that camera—well, it might solve everything for us."

"I still don't see—," Jill began.

"The lens," Greg told her. "I could unscrew the lens of the camera and then I bet I could start a fire by focusing it in the sunlight on some dry bark and stuff. Haven't you ever done that with a magnifying glass and a piece of paper?"

Light dawned at last. "Why yes, of course!" Jill cried. "But I never, never in all the world would have thought of that now. Greg, you had that in your mind all this time, didn't you? I think you're honestly and truly terrific!"

"Well, I haven't found the thing yet and I'm not absolutely sure that it'd work," he answered. "It'll take just the right tinder and a lot of nursing along, too. It'll be as good a gamble, though, as trying to do it by friction—rubbing sticks, you know. In the meantime . . ." He ceased his cutting and reached through the now enlarged hole once again. "Well, the camera isn't in here, but here's the box of chocolate bars, at least. Catch!"

He tossed the box down to Jill. She caught it eagerly, almost overwhelmed by the delicious, heady fragrance that came with it. "Heavens, that smells good!" she exclaimed as Greg hobbled down off the rock pile to join her. "Just take a whiff. Here, you'd better hold it. I don't think I can trust myself with it in my hands. I'll call the boys and tell them that it's found. I wonder what's keeping them out there so long?"

Smiling in anticipation of the twins' delight when they heard the news, Jill stepped to the door. The blanket was still draped over the pine branches, but the boys were nowhere in sight. Only Jody, rousing himself from his long nap but still too heavy from his grisly meal to get up, thumped his tail on the ground in greeting. Jill moved outside and looked around, then called, "Peter! Sam! Boys, where are you?"

Her own voice came back in a mocking echo to her from the walls of the canyon, but there was no other reply. "Sam! Peter!" she shouted more loudly. Her heartbeat quickened while something cold and ominous began to rise within her. "Peter! Sam! Answer me right away. Where are you?" she almost screamed.

The echoes returned, but this time something else, another sound, came with them. "Here we are. Look up here!" a voice called.

At first Jill couldn't tell where the voice had come from because of the reverberations, but at last, high against the cliff across the stream, she caught sight of a movement. Most of the canyon was now in shadow, but sunlight still illumined the upper part of its eastern wall. There, high up and small in the distance, two figures stood on an outcropping of boulders, their hair unmistakeably red in the warm afterglow.

"Look at us! Here we are, way up here," one of them shouted, waving.

"What are you doing up there?" Jill demanded in alarm. "Come on down right away, both of you. We've found the medicine. And the chocolate bars, too," she added as an inducement.

"Oh boy!" one of the twins answered and turned toward where a ledge slanted down along the face of the cliff. "I'll be right there."

The other—it was Sam, Jill thought—stood for another moment, posed cockily with his hands on his hips. Suddenly he began to beat on his chest. "Me Tarzan!" he shouted. "Me—."

The next instant his feet shot out from under him, he fell on his back, and, before Jill could even scream, he came sliding in a shower of sand and gravel over the edge of the boulder and down the steep face of the cliff. Helpless to move or cry out, both her hands pressed tight against her mouth, Jill watched him come. Then, miraculously, his wild descent was halted by the branches of a gnarled old cedar tree that grew out of a cleft halfway down the rock. He seemed to be unharmed, moreover, for he struggled to his feet and was now standing upright on a narrow shelf beside the tree.

At the same moment, Peter appeared again on the boulders far above him, trying to peer over and down. "Sam!" he yelled. "Where are you, Sam?" Even from where she stood below, Jill could see how terrified his face was under its red thatch.

"Get back, Peter," Jill screamed, finding her voice at last. "Get back or you'll fall, too. Sam's all right. A tree stopped him. He's all right, I tell you. Get back from that edge this instant!"

She was conscious, then, that Greg had joined her and now he shouted, too. "Get back, Peter, and come down the way you went up." He fairly roared out the command, and after another moment of hesitation, Peter turned and began to make a slow way back and down along the ledge.

"How about you, Sam? Are you all right? Did you get hurt?" Jill called.

"I'm okay, I guess," Sam answered, but his voice was shaky

"I've got some skinned places and my shirt's torn, but I'm okay."

"Thank goodness!" Jill breathed. Now that it was over she was aware of how her knees were trembling. "And thank goodness for that blessed little tree, too," she added in a lower voice to Greg.

"That's right," he agreed. "Let's thank goodness for it, sure enough. What I'm wondering, though, is how we're going to get Sam down from *there*."

10

Startled by Greg's tone, Jill looked again. Her breath caught and her heart gave a frightened jolt. Yes, the ledge on which Sam stood was really nothing more than a tiny, isolated shelf protruding from the sheer rock wall. What was worse, it so overhung the lower part of the cliff that only emptiness lay between it and a pile of jagged rocks far below. "Oh, Greg!" she whispered. "How far do you suppose it is down from there?"

"A lot too far," he answered. "Thirty feet, I guess, maybe more. And those rocks would sure be bad to land on."

For another long moment the two stood in appalled silence staring up at the figure, so alone and so small on the immense expanse of the cliff. In the stillness they could hear the peaceful sound of the waterfall, the soft, sighing wind in the pines, the twitter of birds preparing for the night, and, now and again, the clatter of stones as Peter moved cautiously down the long slope of the outcropping ledge.

By this time Sam, too, seemed to have recognized his plight. "Say!" he called to them. "I don't see any good way to get down from here, do you? What'll I do?"

"Stay right where you are and don't move any more than you can help," Greg answered quickly. "I've got to figure out the best way to get you down."

"Well, okay, but I wish you'd hurry," Sam said, his round face now plainly worried. "And say, how about those chocolate bars? Don't pass them out until I get there, will you, Jill?"

"I won't," Jill assured him, swallowing down a sudden lump in her throat. "We'll save them until we're all together. Then we'll have a feast."

There was silence again in the canyon while Greg leaned on his crutch, frowning upward at the rocky wall. Jill waited for him to speak, while inside her that familiar dark, bleak coldness had begun to grow and take shape again, filling her chest so that her heart pounded heavily and it was hard for her to breathe. Her mouth grew dry and there was a queer, metallic taste in it. No, it's no use, she found herself thinking, in despair. Sam will have to stay up there until help comes, and when will that be? Meanwhile—? The night will be so cold, and on that wind-swept ledge—.

She remembered accounts she had read in newspapers about people lost in these mountains. "The victim evidently died of exposure," they so often ended. Or Sam might easily fall asleep during the long night hours and slip off. She screwed her eyes tight shut, trying to blot out the picture that leaped into her mind, the picture of Sam sliding down, as before, in a shower of stones and gravel. But this time there would be no tree to save him, nothing but those terrible, jagged rocks waiting there below.

And only a few minutes ago I was actually beginning to think of this as an exciting adventure, even making up romantic dreams about Greg and me. However could I be so shallow and heartless, with Mrs. Wendell and poor Dr. Curry maybe lying dead all the while? And now this has happened. It seems as though there really is something cruel and hostile looming over us among these mountains, watching and waiting, ready to swoop down and punish us for forgetting for a single instant to be afraid of it.

Her thoughts were interrupted by Peter, down at last, who came running toward them across the wide expanse of the creek bed. The twins had arranged stepping stones between the sand bars, but now in his hurry, Peter came splashing heedlessly through the water. "Golly!" he exclaimed as he joined them. "Look at where Sam is! If that tree hadn't stopped him he'd have been killed for sure, wouldn't he?"

Jill could only nod in reply. Then, "Oh, Peter!" she said. "What in the world made you climb up there in the first place?" As though that mattered now, she thought, as soon as the words were out.

"The lower part of that ledge is where the wild strawberries are," he explained. "We went up there, first of all, to—well, to see how they were coming along. Then we noticed how the ledge slanted on upward and we wondered if we could maybe get to the top of the canyon on it. It only goes as far as those boulders, though. It was Sam who had that idea," he added, defensively.

"It doesn't matter whose it was, it was a perfectly crazy notion and you both ought—ought—!" Helpless anger suddenly overwhelmed Jill.

"Golly, I'm sorry," Peter said. "But say, Greg, how do you suppose Sam's going to get down? A fireman's ladder could reach him, but I don't believe they could get a fire truck in here, not with the road so washed out, could they? Maybe they'll have to bring in a helicopter. What do you think, Greg?"

"Either a ladder truck or a helicopter would be helpful," Greg said, smiling wryly. "The trouble is, neither one's available right now."

"Well, a helicopter came over here this morning, didn't it, Jill? If it comes tomorrow it'll see our S.O.S. sign, and we can tell it to get Sam off first," Peter's eyes were beginning to sparkle. "Then it can lift the rest of us out, afterwards. Boy! I've always wanted to ride in a helicopter!"

"And have Sam sit up on that little shelf all night?" Greg said, shaking his head.

Peter looked disappointed. "Well, I guess we'll just have to haul him up with a rope, then," he said.

"A rope would be helpful, too," Greg agreed. "Except that I haven't seen one around, either."

"How about the clothesline, Jill?" Peter asked. "You had it yesterday. You were hanging dish towels on it."

"The clothesline—and the trees it was tied to—are gone," Jill told him. "But—" an idea had come to her. "We could make a rope of blankets, couldn't we? Those new cotton blankets we found in the cupboard would be good and strong. Tied together, they would reach him—there are six of them. Oh, Greg, wouldn't that work?" Hope had sprung alive in her.

Greg's face cleared a little. "Yes, it might," he agreed. "It'd be strong enough to hold him, all right. But as for hauling him up, I wonder. It would have to be from those boulders above him. Is there any place there to brace oneself to pull even Sam's weight? I'll have to go up and have a look at it before I can tell."

"But Greg, how can you climb that ledge with your ankle?" Jill began.

"I can do it if I have to," Greg answered shortly. "Meanwhile, let's get the blankets out and make the rope, anyway."

"I'll get them," Peter offered.

"It'll take two of us to carry them," Jill said. "I'll have a look at Betsey while I'm there. You stay here, Greg. I think one of us should be here to watch Sam and talk to him. We don't want him to get panicky up there alone."

"I'll stay," Greg agreed.

On the way to the cabin Jill noticed the big wool blanket still stretched out to dry and she gathered it up hastily, pausing only to shake the sand out of it. Betsey was still asleep, she was relieved to see. She seemed to be breathing more easily, too, although her cheeks were still deeply flushed. Jill and Peter picked up the other blankets and took them out to where Greg was waiting, followed now by Jody, who had roused himself at last from his torpid sleep.

"Shouldn't we cut them into strips?" Jill asked. "They'll be easier to tie if they aren't so wide."

"Better tie them by the corners, anyway," Greg said. "But it would be a good idea, at that, to split them down the middle, lengthwise. They'll still be plenty strong and there'll be more of them—to make a longer rope if we need it."

With only Peter's jackknife to work with, cutting the blankets down the center was a laborious job. Greg tried to tear them, but they wouldn't rip lengthwise. "Well, that shows that they are plenty tough, anyway, and that's all to the good," he said, and resumed the job of sawing them apart with the knife.

By now blue shadows were gathering in the depths of the canyon, although there was still a glow of sunlight where Sam was perched. With the shadows came a breeze, light at first, but blowing steadily and bringing a warning of the evening's chill. Jill felt herself shivering as she worked at fastening the corners of the blankets together, tying them carefully with firm, square knots. Once she looked up to see how Sam was faring. He was sitting down now, close against the tree, his arms huddled around his knees. Oh dear, he's cold already,

113

Jill thought, noting how the branches of the cedar, beside him, were moving in the wind.

When Greg had finished cutting the blankets he, too, looked up at Sam, and Jill saw his brows draw together. "We'd better get started. It's going to get dark a lot too soon," he said. He picked up the long string of blankets and went over the knots, jerking at each of them to test it. Jill watched him, almost breathless in suspense for fear he might find fault with her work, but at the end he gave her a quick, approving grin. "Fine!" he said. "You must have been a Girl Scout. Not a granny among them. Well, here we go."

"Wait, Greg," Jill said. "I still don't think you should try to climb that narrow ledge on your crutch. It's too dangerous. Let me do it. If you should fall—!" She could almost feel herself turn pale at that thought.

"I won't fall," he said. "And I won't use my crutch, I'll crawl. I did that before and covered quite a distance, remember? Besides, there's the question of hauling Sam up, you know."

"Yes, I've been thinking about that, too. Couldn't Peter and I, together, do it? I'm really pretty strong, and there'd be two of us."

Greg's eyes crinkled in a smile, but he was shaking his head when Peter broke in. "I'm real strong, too," Peter said. "I've got good muscles, the best muscles in our Cub Scout den. Mr. Harris, our leader, measured them and said so," and he flexed his biceps proudly.

"Listen, you two," Greg said. "I'm not a bit sure that all three of us, working together, will be able to haul Sam up. We certainly can't unless there's some good way to brace ourselves there, and from here it doesn't look to me as though there is. What I'm going up there for is to find out. Now suppose you and Peter help me by wrapping this blanket thing around me so that I'll have both arms and hands free to climb."

"But—" Peter began. A look from Greg silenced him, however, and he joined Jill in winding the long string of blankets around Greg. They were awkward and bulky, and by the time they were all on him, he looked almost as wide as he was tall.

Sam had been watching their preparations with increasing impatience and concern. "Say, what's going on?" he demanded, standing up to see better.

"I'm coming up the ledge to those boulders above you and I'm taking this rope of blankets along to let down to you from there," Greg told him, and Sam settled back, satisfied.

"Are you sure you don't want me to come with you?" Jill asked. "I might be able to help."

Greg shook his head again. "No, you'll have to stay down here to tell me whether or not I'm getting the rope within Sam's reach when I let it down. I don't think I'll be able to see him from up there and I'll need someone to guide me. Well, here I go."

He hobbled briskly across the creek and to the foot of the slanting ledge, then left his crutch and began the ascent on his hands and knees. Jill watched him anxiously, and even Peter seemed to realize how difficult the climb would be for him in that manner. "The ledge is pretty narrow up above there," he said. "I sure hope he can make it."

"He will. He can do *anything*," Jill answered. She was not nearly so sure as she sounded, but she had a feeling that if she expressed her confidence firmly enough it would in some way help him.

"Yes, I guess he can," Peter said, nodding. "He's sure a swell guy, that Greg." He moved close against Jill's side as he spoke, she put an arm around his shoulders and they stood together, their eyes fixed on the two figures on the wall of the canyon while Jody, sensing that something was worrying them, whined in sympathy. Where Greg was the shadows were thick, and even Sam's high perch was no longer in the sun. Darkness would be upon them soon, and after that, the long, cold, hostile night.

Jill shut her eyes and whispered a little prayer to herself, but opened them with a grasp of fright at the sound of stones rattling down. Both boys were all right, however, and she saw that Greg had made good progress, hampered though he was by the bulky roll of blankets. He was already more than half-way up the sloping ledge.

"Now comes the bad part," Peter said. "It'll be worse with all that stuff wrapped around him. He won't be able to keep as flat against the rocks as we could."

Greg had evidently recognized the difficulty, and they saw him pause for a moment. Then, instead of crawling, he rose to his knees and sidled slowly and carefully along the ledge with his face to the canyon wall.

"There!" Peter exclaimed with a sigh of relief. "He's made it. Well, we knew he would, didn't we?"

"Of course we did," Jill agreed, but she, too, let out a long, quivering breath.

Now Greg had reached the boulders. They saw him unwind the blankets from around himself and crawl out upon the rocks, trying to look over the edge and down to where Sam was.

"Oh, Greg, be careful! That's where Sam slipped!" Jill called to him.

"Don't worry, I'm careful," he answered. "It's the way I figured. I can't see Sam without going out farther than I dare. I'll have to let the rope down from where I am. Keep holding on to the tree, Sam, and don't try to reach the rope until it's right where you are. Don't let go of the tree for even a second, no matter what. Understand? Here it comes."

The gray pile poised for a moment on the edge of the boulders, then slowly slid forward and went streaming down over them like a strange, deliberate waterfall. Sam stood up eagerly to watch it come. "It's plenty long enough," Jill called, but even as she spoke, she saw a gust of wind catch the blanket-rope and sway it away from Sam's ledge to well beyond his grasp. When it swung back in a momentary lessening of the breeze it caught on a rocky projection and hung there, still too far to one side for him to reach.

"How did it go?" Greg shouted down from where he was holding the upper end. "Have you got it, Sam?"

"No!" Sam answered. "It's stuck way over there on some rocks."

"The wind blew it off to Sam's right," Jill called. "It swung back, but then it caught on something. Jerk it a little and see if it'll come loose and swing back to him. It's plenty long enough, anyway."

Greg pulled the blanket-rope up and down a few times, but by the time it had swung free, the wind was blowing even more strongly and steadily and the blanket streamed out again far away from Sam's ledge. "Golly!" Peter said. "He can't get it to him, after all!"

"How's it doing now?" Greg shouted down again.

"The wind's still blowing it way over to the right," Jill answered. "Greg, I think you'll have to weight the end of it, somehow."

"Okay, I'll tie a rock in that corner," Greg said, and began to haul the long, irregular line up again. Those below saw him working at it while the breeze increased and the darkness grew. Then he piled the gray mass once again on the edge of the boulders. "Listen, Sam," he called. "I had to use a pretty big rock to make sure it'll hang straight down. You keep as far back against the wall of the cliff as you can to make sure it doesn't hit you. I'll let it down slowly, but it may swing. Understand?"

"Sure!" Sam answered. "I hope it works, this time. It's getting awfully cold here."

Slowly, the knotted gray line of blankets crept down the cliff. Twilight was deepening, but Jill could see clearly enough to know that, although it swayed a little, it was going straight down to where the boy waited. Suddenly Sam gave a whoop of triumph. "Yea! I've got it!" he shouted. "I've got hold of it okay, Greg. What'll I do now?"

"Untie the end and get the rock out," Greg directed. "How are you at knots, Sam? Can you tie a half hitch?"

"Sure, that's an easy one. I've done a hundred of them in Scouts."

"Fine. When you've got the rock out, wind your end around the trunk of that cedar tree, as near its base as you can. Wind it at least twice around and then tie it with two good half hitches. When it's fast I'll let down my end."

"But Greg," Jill called, interposing. "What use is it for him to tie it to the tree? Shouldn't he tie it around himself, instead, so we can haul him up?"

"No, this'll have to be the way, Jill," Greg answered. "I'm not much of an engineer, but even I can tell that we can't pull him up over these boulders. The rope would almost surely slip into a crevice between them and wedge itself, once his weight was on it."

"But what can we do?" Jill faltered.

"Sam will have to let himself down the rope," Greg said. "How about it, boy? You've slid down ropes before, haven't you? This'll be nice and easy on the hands—and, with all those knots to grip on, it ought to be a cinch for any good Scout."

11

Sam's reply came promptly. "Sure I've slid down a lot of ropes," he declared. "Shall I start right now?"

"No, wait," Greg told him. "Wait until I get down below so I can hold the rope steady for you."

"Okay, I'll wait, but hurry. It's getting awfully cold up here, and it's dark, too," Sam said, and Jill could hear a slight tremor in his voice.

It seemed to take Greg a long while to make his way back down along the shadowy ledge. Jill and Peter crossed the stream and were waiting with growing anxiety for him at the foot of the cliff, when he came hobbling up the pile of rocks to join them. "Is that rope tied good and tight, Sam?" he called as soon as he arrived.

"Sure, just like you said. Twice around the tree and then two half hitches," Sam answered. Here, close to the cliff, the echoes were different, and his voice seemed to come from very far away.

"Let down the rope, then," Greg directed.

The long, knotted blanket-rope came tumbling down upon them and hung there, swaying like a tall pillar of gray mist in the gray half-light. "Now I'm going to give this thing a try, Sam," Greg called upward. "I want you to watch that cedar tree, especially its roots, while I pull on the rope to make sure it's going to hold you. Understand?"

"Sure," Sam answered again.

Greg handed his crutch to Jill, grasped the end of the rope, and swung his weight upon it. "How was that?" he asked.

"It holds, all right," Sam's voice reached them jubilantly through the dimness. "*Now* can I slide down?"

"Come ahead. I'll hold this end as steady as I can so you won't swing too much," Greg told him.

"Oh, Sam, be sure to grip the rope hard between your feet, too," Jill added anxiously. "And take it slowly all the way down. Don't let go until your feet touch down here. These rocks will be mean to land on, even from a short distance."

"Sure, I know all that stuff. Well, here goes!" Sam shouted.

Jill strained her eyes upward through the glimmering twilit air to watch the small figure as it moved down the long, swaying line. Oh, he's coming a lot too fast, she thought, and caught her underlip in her teeth. Part way down, however, Sam seemed to get better control, and his landing was easy and light.

"Say, how did I do? Pretty neat, wasn't it?" he asked, grinning around at them.

"Good enough for an amateur," Greg told him.

Jody was already greeting his long-lost master with ecstatic jumps and frantic tail-waggings. Peter didn't say anything. Instead, he began to punch his twin gently in the stomach, repeating the gesture over and over as though he liked the feel of him under his fist once again. Jill found Sam's cockiness a little hard to take after all their anxiety, but her relief was so vast that she would have engulfed him in a hug if he hadn't fended her off. She shook his hand, anyway, feeling a momentary pang at its icy coldness. His face, too, looked pinched and chilly, in spite of his impudent grin, and his nose was running. My goodness, I hope *he* hasn't caught a cold, Jill thought.

"Well, what's for dinner?" he demanded. "Boy, am I hungry! And say, how about all those chocolate bars?"

Back in the cabin, they found Betsey sitting up in the bunk. "Where have all of you been?" she demanded.

"We've been getting Sam down off the cliff where he had himself stuck," Peter told her.

"Whatever did you do that for, Sam?" Betsey asked him, wide-eyed. Sam didn't seem to have any answer ready, so she changed the subject. "I feel lots better. I'm all well," she announced, scrambling out of the bunk. "But I still need some cough medicine," she added, quickly.

"It's time for our supper. You can have your medicine afterwards, before you go to bed," Jill told her. She produced the cans and the box of chocolate bars. "Which can shall we open?" she asked. "The chocolate will be our dessert."

"Any one will do. It won't matter what's in it, just so it's eatable," Peter said. "We'll have the chocolate to look forward to, even if it turns out to be squash again."

Greg took the can outside, where the light was a little better, and they all surrounded him while he pounded it open with record speed. This time it was roast-beef hash!

"Our luck's sure changed at last!" Peter exulted.

Never had anything smelled so spicily appetizing or tasted so delicious. Jill offered Jody a small portion of her share, but he seemed uninterested, so she ate it gratefully herself. As for the chocolate bars, when she handed out one to each member of the party, they were received in almost reverent silence. "Eat them slowly so they'll last longer," Jill said as she peeled the wrappings from her own.

By the time the last crumb was finished and every finger licked thriftily clean, the canyon was deep in shadow and stars were beginning to appear, large and luminous in the narrow strip of sky. The wind had increased and it soon became so cold that they moved inside the cabin for shelter. "I can go to bed now, if I have my medicine," Betsey volunteered.

The twins had already climbed into their bunk. Jill found her own eyelids all at once so heavy she could barely keep them open. "It's been a busy day!" she said to Greg when the youngsters were settled. "How's your ankle? Would you like me to tie it up again?"

"Yes, if you don't mind. It doesn't hurt too much, but I got a lot of sand inside the bandage when I crawled along the ledge. It'll help to get it out."

Jill removed the bandage carefully, shook it out, then bound the ankle up again. "There you are," she said. "It's getting colder, isn't it? I'm sorry we have only the one blanket apiece, after all. Those that we had to leave hanging out there on the cliff would have come in handy tonight, wouldn't they?"

"That's right," Greg agreed. "But say, I've been wondering. There are only three bunks for the five of us. Shall I clear out another one for you?"

"Oh, no. We all four slept in the upper ones last night," Jill explained. "I—I thought we'd be safer up there. I slept with Betsey, and I can again. It makes it warmer for two of us to be together, sharing the blanket. And I had Jody in with me, too."

"Jody? Why him?"

"Well, after I got in my bunk, I began to worry about him down on the floor, alone. You see this place is open to the whole outdoors, and I had heard coyotes the night before. And, of course, there was that mountain lion."

"Mountain lion!" Greg exclaimed. "Around here?"

When Jill told him how they had seen the creature twice, Greg whistled softly. "You've been having your problems right along. Mountain lions, though—you really don't need to be too afraid of them. That is, if you leave them alone. Down in South America, in fact, they call them 'The Christian's Friend.' They say that in the mountains there they hang around camps just to watch the people, real friendly and curious, and never attack men."

"South America? Have you been there?" Jill asked, suddenly wide-awake again.

"Sure. Our family's been living in Chile for the last five years. My dad's an engineer up at a mine in the mountains there. They sent me back to this country this spring to get ready for college. That's how I met Dr. Curry." He broke off, and when he continued his voice sounded strained, as though he were thinking once more of the tragedy. "He's been tutoring me for the exams. We took this trip for a sort of vacation after they were over."

"I see," Jill said, her own throat tightening in sympathy. I ought to change the subject, she thought. We mustn't talk about Dr. Curry or—or Mrs. Wendell, either. Making an extra effort, she spoke again. "You know, Greg, we've been here working hard together all day long and we really don't know a thing about each other except our names. Where have you been living since you came back to this country?"

"In Dr. Curry's apartment, near the University," he answered. "How about you? Where do you live?"

"We live near the beach," she said. "I have an older sister named Beth and an older brother named Rick. My father's a lawyer. Beth goes to college in Santa Barbara and Rick will be a senior in high school next year. I'm in high school, too— a sophomore. I came here on this baby-sitting job because my friend, Phoebe Walker, who was supposed to come, fell downstairs and fractured her arm, and I wanted to hold the job for her. She's awfully clever and ambitious. She's planning to be a doctor." Her voice trailed off.

Now it seemed to be Greg's turn to make conversation. "So you're the baby of the family, are you? Well, I have three brothers and two sisters, all younger than I am. My brothers' names are Don, Jack, and Steve, and my sisters are Patty and Ellen. So that's that, and now I think we're properly introduced, don't you? How about some shut-eye? I'm pretty beat, myself. The kids are all fed and tucked in and not much can happen to them tonight, seems to me. Besides, our luck's changed now, definitely changed, as Peter said. We found the medicine and the chocolate bars, got Sam down, Betsey's better, and we had roast-beef hash for supper. Once we find that camera—"

"Oh, don't say it out loud!" Jill exclaimed, glancing fearfully over her shoulder at the dark, yawning doorway.

Greg peered at her sharply. "What's the matter? Who's going to hear me?"

Jill felt her cheeks turning hot and she was glad of the dimness so that he could not see them. "Nobody, I suppose. It's just—just that I can't help the feeling that there's something—something out there . . ."

"Are you superstitious?" Greg demanded.

"No, not really." She hesitated again. "But Greg, every time we seem to be getting a break another dreadful thing happens. Like the blue jay taking our matches, and the rattlesnake, and Betsey getting sick, and then Sam, stuck on the cliff—. It's as though there were something cruel and powerful in these mountains that's our enemy and doesn't want us to escape." The words came hurriedly, now, pouring out in spite of herself. "Something that's listening and watching and waiting to pounce again, if we get hopeful and confident. Like a cat playing with a mouse," she ended, in an unhappy whisper.

"Say, you've sure got a lot of imagination—a lot too much for comfort, my girl!" Greg said. "Imagination's fine, but not when you let it run away with you. Put all that fool stuff out of your head, beginning right now, and up into that bunk with you! Things'll look brighter in the morning. Wait and see."

Jill climbed silently into her bunk. Oh, why did I ever tell Greg all that, she asked herself. What an utter idiot he must think me! Still, telling him had been a relief, for her mind seemed more at ease, and all at once she felt sleepy again. She lay down beside the small, warm bundle that was Betsey and drew the blanket over them both.

Remembering something, she sat up. "Greg," she called. "What about Jody? Will you lift him up here to me, please?"

"No, your bunk's crowded enough already. I'll take him in with me. Besides, he'll make a good heating pad for me," he added, with a chuckle.

"Well then, thank you, and good night."

"Good night, sleep tight," he answered, and Jill settled down once more. Greg's really *kind* she thought. Kind, besides everything else that's terrific. But, oh dear, he's ready for the University and I'm only a sophomore in high school. He's traveled so much and I've never been anywhere. He probably thinks of me as just another child, like the twins! I'm fifteen, but he's surely eighteen at least. That's three years difference.

Well, three years may seem like a lot, but it isn't much more than the difference between me and Rod, and *he* said he was going to ask me for a date, she reminded herself. My goodness, how upset I was at having to come away up here just after that! Yet it was really lucky, because if I hadn't come I'd never have met—.

Appalled, she stopped herself. There I go again! It's wrong even to think *anything's* lucky about it, after what's probably happened to two fine people. But still, Greg *is* nice, and hav-

125

ing him here makes everything seem so much better. Surely it can't do any harm to think *that*.

She heard Greg climbing into the lower bunk. There was a scrambling noise as he brought Jody in, too, and the little dog made a place for himself. Jill was conscious of a new transparency in the shadows and the rectangles of the doorway and the open end of the cabin grew plainer. The moon's risen, she thought. It must be almost full tonight.

The knowledge that Greg was there below her made the darkness and cold, the enormous, brooding emptiness around them, even a coyote's weird and ghostly quaverings, seem infinitely less menacing. She drew a long, deep breath, turned over, and went to sleep.

The sun, shining into the cabin, woke Jill at last. She sat up and Betsey stirred briefly beside her, then settled down again. The little girl looked rosy from sleep, but there was no more of the feverish flush and her forehead felt cool under Jill's anxious touch. That's something to be thankful for already, Jill thought.

She looked over at the still-formidably-large pile of sand, rocks, and gravel which blocked the drawers and the closet door. We'll have to clear all that away as fast as we can, she thought. There's only three cans of food left, along with the chocolate bars. We *have* to find that camera today. Even after we find it and Greg gets the lens out, there's still the problem of starting the fire. Will it really work? She recalled how easy it was to burn holes in paper with her father's big reading glass, but would a little camera lens serve the same purpose? What could they use for fuel to get the fire started? Thin pieces of dried bark and maybe pine needles, gathered from above the floodline, since they had no paper.

Suddenly she was scrambling out of the bunk and down the ladder. She had remembered the pile of old magazines in the top cupboard. They were a little damp, but they'd soon dry in the sun.

Neither Greg nor Jody was in the lower bunk, but she could hear someone moving outside, and now a shadow filled the doorway. "Good morning!" Greg said.

"Oh, Greg, I've just thought of something," Jill told him, eagerly. "Those old magazines up in the top cupboard. They're only a little damp. I can put them out in the sun and they'll be wonderful to start our fire with when we find the camera. I'll take them outdoors right this minute so they'll be good and dry."

"That's a good idea," he agreed. "Jody and I've been looking around for fuel. There's plenty, once we get the fire actually started, but dry paper will sure help in the beginning. That is, *if* we find the camera."

"Oh, we've got to find it!" Jill cried. "That camera has to be somewhere in there, it simply has to."

"The camera? *My* camera?" Peter was looking down at them from his bunk. "What about my camera?"

When Greg explained his plan, Peter looked none too pleased. "But I don't want you to take the lens out. What good's a camera without a lens? That would spoil it, for sure, even if the water hasn't already. It's a fine camera—it really takes pictures—and I've got a flashbulb holder, too. I don't want my camera wrecked, no sir!"

"Just unscrewing the lens for a while won't wreck it, Peter," Jill assured him. "It can be put back afterwards. You see, building a fire is our very best chance of attracting help. The fire wardens are always on the lookout for smoke in these mountains and they'll notice ours, never fear. They'll send a plane over to see what's making it and then they'll see our sign—the S.O.S. that you boys made."

"Say, that's right." Peter's face brightened. "Maybe they'll send a helicopter to get us out. I'd sure like that."

"How's Sam?" Jill asked. "Is he all right this morning?"

"Hey, Sam, you okay?" Peter demanded. There was an indistinguishable mutter from Sam. "He says he's asleep," Peter translated. "Well, I'm not and I sure am hungry. What's for breakfast? Besides chocolate bars, I mean?"

12

Breakfast brought the problem of which can to open. "Not the sardines." Jill begged. Hungry though she was, the idea of sardines and chocolate for breakfast was more than she could face.

That left a choice between the two cylindrical cans, one much larger than the other. "Since we have the chocolate, too, we'd better use the smaller one," Jill suggested.

While Greg opened the can, Jill got the stack of old magazines down from the high cupboard and took them outside to dry. She propped them open on a flat rock, with stones between the leaves so that the sun and wind could reach every page. There are eight of them, she noted. Surely with so much paper and plenty of wood we can soon have a good fire going—*if* we find the camera and *if* the lens will really ignite them.

The can proved to contain applesauce, and everyone agreed that this was another stroke of good luck. Topped off with a chocolate bar apiece, it made a reasonably satisfying break-fast, and they were all in good spirits when they began once again to clear away the pile of debris.

The job went far more slowly than it had before, however, for the pile had, of course, been smaller at its top. To reach a lower level there was a lot more of it to remove. As the sun rose higher the inside of the cabin grew warm. Jill found herself beginning to tire under the fast pace Greg set, while the twins paused more and more often to rest. At last, when they had dug enough away to reach one of the drawers, they found in it nothing but bath towels and pillowcases, all of them muddy and wet.

"Well, I might as well hang some of these out to dry. Then, when the sand's shaken out of them, we'll at least have a towel apiece to use, and that will be nice for a change," Jill said, trying to sound cheerful as she gathered up a soggy arm-ful. There was no response from the others, who all looked disheartened and glum.

Outside, with the breeze cooling her hot face, Jill draped the towels over the tree branches. It was a beautiful morning, she couldn't help noticing. Birds were singing in the willows and a blue jay, perched on a near-by branch, cocked his head at her and gave an inquiring squawk. "No, I've nothing for you—and even if I had, I wouldn't give you any, not after your stealing our precious matches," Jill told him, severely.

Just then an all-too-familiar shadow glided past her along the ground and Jill looked up to see, once again, the sinister, wide-winged birds circling slowly, black against the blue sky. She felt the same chilly shiver between her shoulder blades, in spite of the sun's warmth, and hurried back inside the cabin.

"Let's see, there were two sets of drawers, three deep, on each side of the closet door," she said, trying to speak with a cheerfulness she did not feel. "Or were there four? I can't recall for sure. I do remember, though, that we put the boys' clothing in the drawers on the left side of the door. Maybe your mother laid the camera in with your things, Peter. What do you think?"

"Golly, I don't know," Peter said, wiping his sweaty face with his forearm and leaving still another muddy streak across it. "No telling where she put it. Maybe it's hanging by its strap in that closet. That's where I kept it at home—in my closet."

There was a dismayed silence at this news, for it was plain to them all that the closet door couldn't be opened until the whole vast pile was moved out of the way. "This isn't a bit of fun any more," Betsey announced, finally. She had been working hard in her own fashion, but actually getting in the others' way a good deal. "I'd rather go outside and dig for cans like we did before. Let's go and do that, Jill."

"There just aren't any more cans there to dig for, I'm afraid," Jill explained. "This work is more important now, Betsey."

"Well, I'm tired of it. I'm going out and throw sticks for Jody. I know he's lonesome for me."

"All right, honey, but don't go away from the house," Jill said. "Don't forget that rattlesnake."

"He's dead, silly, and Jody ate him all up," Betsey reminded her.

"Yes," Greg put in. "But there might be others around. He probably had a family. Stay right there in front where we can keep an eye on you. I don't want anything else to happen to my very best girl."

"Okay, Greg," Betsey answered, giving him her special smile.

The next drawer, opened at last, was full of the boys' clothes, all of them wet and muddy. But no camera! Jill carried a change of garments for each twin out to dry, glad of the chance for another few minutes rest for her aching muscles. Betsey was still playing with Jody, but when Jill appeared she paused. "I'm hungry, Jill. When's lunch?"

Jill looked at her watch. "It's only ten o'clock, Betsey. We still have lots of work to do. It's not time to be hungry, yet."

"Well, I am, anyway, and so's Jody. He didn't have any breakfast at all, remember?"

And so am I hungry, too, Jill thought, conscious now of a very definite hollowness inside her. Back in the cabin, she spoke to Greg. "It's ten o'clock. Maybe we should stop for a rest and a drink. At least there's plenty of water. Will you fill the pitcher, boys?"

When the twins were out of earshot she turned to Greg again. "What do you think of the idea of having a piece of chocolate—not a whole bar, but a piece—too? I read somewhere that people don't get so hungry if they eat small bits of food often, instead of big meals hours apart."

"*Big* meals?" He cocked an eyebrow at her. "Who's been having them? But maybe you're right. Let's try it, anyway."

The water and the slowly nibbled chocolate, as well as the chance to rest, gave the laborers some new energy. Greg, however, paused only briefly. "The sun doesn't shine directly down into this canyon after the middle of the afternoon. Unless we find the lens while the sun's good and strong, we won't be able to make it work today," he explained.

The rest of this day and then tonight and maybe another day, with only the two cans and the few chocolate bars left, Jill thought. And if we can't find the camera, after all—?

It was clear that the twins had sensed the problem, too, for they looked soberly from Greg to each other and back again. Suddenly Sam's face brightened. "Say! How about those wild strawberries? There were a few that looked as though they might be ripe today. Come on, Pete, let's go have a look."

"Good! Better get them before the birds do," Greg said. "But don't go climbing any farther, remember."

They hurried off with the basket, and for a while Greg and Jill worked silently, both of them full of their own worried thoughts. "Greg," Jill said, at last. "What if—what if we can't find the lens? Or what if it won't work, after all, even if we do find it?"

"I've been thinking about that, too. In that case, I'll climb up out of the canyon and go for help myself. I'll start in the late afternoon and get as far as I can in the night while it's cool. The moon's full, or nearly. It'll be bright enough to see by. In the daytime I'll take it easy, even lie up under the shade of a bush if it gets too hot. I'll take some of that red cloth to signal with if a plane comes over."

"But your ankle!" Jill protested. Black, aching misery had come flooding through her at the thought of his leaving. And what about him? Alone on those rugged, sun-scorched slopes, crippled, without water? How could he hope to find his way among the tangles of chapparal that weren't high enough or thick enough to give real shade yet were so difficult to see through? Suddenly, with dreadful clarity, she could see the circling buzzards. "Oh, Greg, no!" she whispered. "No, you *mustn't!*"

"Sure I must. Listen, Jill, it'll be the only thing left to do. It's what I'd have tried at the very first if it hadn't been for my ankle. That's really a lot better today, and by tomorrow night it ought to have improved some more."

"No, you mustn't," Jill still insisted, shaking her head. "Professor Wendell will be coming by the end of next week, anyway." She faltered, then continued. "We must stick together, right here, all of us. You just mustn't try it. If anything should happen to you—" She couldn't go on.

"Hey, take it easy! No sense in getting worked up before

133

it happens. And maybe it won't, after all. We still have a good chance of finding that—"

He was interrupted by a burst of barking from Jody and the sound of running feet. An instant later, the twins dashed into the cabin, both so out of breath that for a moment they could only point excitedly behind them. "What's the matter?" Jill cried. "What's happened?"

"A bear!" Peter gasped. "There was a bear up on the ledge, a real bear!"

"A black bear," Sam said. "He was eating our wild strawberries. *Our* strawberries!"

"A bear!" Betsey, who had followed them inside, gave a terrified scream and rushed into Jill's arms. "Is it chasing you? Don't let it eat *me*, Jill. Make it go away! Make it go away!" She hid her face against Jill, who clutched her tightly, while Greg grabbed up his crutch and began to climb down off the pile of gravel.

"Don't worry, silly, he's gone off up the canyon," Sam said. "But he ate our strawberries, like I told you, and he even spoiled all the rest of them that weren't ripe. I wish I'd had a gun. I'd have shot him dead right then and there. I threw a rock at him, but it didn't hit him and then he ran away."

"Oh my goodness!" Jill said, appalled. "You don't mean you threw a rock at a wild bear? Oh, Sam, he might have attacked you. Don't you know how dangerous bears can be out in the woods. Especially if you bother them when they're eating?"

"Well, he made me mad, eating our strawberries," Sam said. "I just wish I *had* hit him, that's all."

"I guess you're pretty lucky that you didn't," Greg said. "Who knows, maybe he thought they were *his* strawberries. It *is* too bad about them, though. I had thought of birds taking them, but I never thought of bears. Remember this, Sam, never get into an argument with a bear out in the open. Wait until he's in a zoo and there are good strong iron bars between you."

Greg was smiling now, but Jill could see that his face was paler than it had been before. As for herself, she felt drained and weak-kneed as she held Betsey tight against her. Bears! On top of everything else, bears! What next?

"Okay, I'll remember," Sam said, but he sounded unconvinced. "What time is it now, Jill? Is it time for lunch yet? I'm sure hungry!"

"So am I," Peter agreed, while Betsey put in an eager "Me too!"

Jill looked questioningly at Greg and saw him shake his head. "Let's see, what time is it?" she said and looked at her watch. "For heavens' sake, it's only half past eleven. Not even noon yet, not nearly time for lunch. Come on, get to work, you three. There's all of this still to dig out."

Sam turned reluctantly to the job. "Okay, but I really am hungry. Last night I kept dreaming about food. I dreamed we were having bacon and waffles for breakfast and I could smell them cooking. But just before I began to eat them, I woke up."

"What kept waking me up was my stomach sort of churning around and growling out loud," Peter said. "I could hear Sam's, too, right next to me. First mine, then his—boy, what a racket!"

" 'Their rumblings abdominal were something phenomenal,' " Greg quoted, chuckling, but the humor was lost on the youngsters, and he had to translate the long words for them.

"I guess that's funny," Peter said, uncertainly. "But it isn't so funny when you feel it."

If we're all so hungry now, with what we've been having to eat, how will it be by the end of next week with no more cans and nothing else in sight? Jill asked herself as she worked on. Not only her back and arms were aching, but the blisters on her palms had opened and the raw surfaces stung sharply. She looked down at them, then at her grimy, broken-off nails. What a mess I am, she thought. I suppose my face is just as dirty as the twins', and as for my hair—! Oh, well, what's the use? I'll just have to make myself stop thinking of how I look and concentrate on what really matters: digging out this dirt. Maybe working hard will help keep my mind off food. Although, on the other hand, the exercise will probably make me hungrier than ever!

By this time, they had cleared the front of another drawer. Greg pulled it open and they all hurried to peer inside. "Those are my clothes," Betsey announced. "There's my new red sweater."

Greg rummaged quickly through the contents. "No camera," he said in a flat voice and wiped his hand across his forehead.

How tired he looks! Jill thought with a pang. And no wonder—balancing on one foot and digging so hard all this while. Or is it the shadow of his beard that gives that hollow look to his cheeks? Of course he's old enough to be shaving, and he hasn't had a chance to for these three days.

Betsey's clothes, like all the other things at this level, were wet and muddy, and, what was more, dye from the red sweater had streaked and colored everything else. "Well, the sweater'll be nice and warm for you tonight, anyway," Jill said, and carried it out to add to the assortment drying on the tree.

While she was draping it carefully over a branch, something bright green in the stream near the willow caught her eye and she went over to see what it was. "Why, it's water cress!" she exclaimed aloud. Yes, I'm sure that's what it is. We have it often at home, in salads. So it's edible. Stooping, she plucked a sprig and nibbled at it cautiously. The fresh, peppery tang was unmistakable.

Quickly she gathered a big bunch, rinsed it off under the waterfall and carried it back in triumph. "Here's a treat!" she announced. "A fine green salad for us, fresh-picked water cress! You don't get it this fresh, ever, in the markets at home. Here, try some."

"Say, that's fine!" Greg's face lit up. The three younger ones seemed less impressed. "It looks just like old weeds to me," Sam said. "Is it really okay to eat it?"

"Yes, we have it in salad all the time at home," Jill assured him. "And there's plenty of it under the willows. We can have all we want."

First Sam, then Peter, finally Betsey tasted the green leaves. "Well, it wouldn't be too bad with plenty of mayonnaise on it," Sam said grudgingly. Peter made a face and so did Betsey, although when she saw that Greg was eating his with evident enjoyment, she tasted hers again. "I like it, it's good," she said. "Me and Greg both like it, but I still like chocolate better."

The cress was pleasant to munch on while they set to their labors once more. "It's got lots of vitamins in it," Jill told them, putting all the enthusiasm she could muster into her voice.

"And no calories, that's for sure," Greg added.

By this time, the dump of sand and gravel and rocks outside the doorway was almost as big as the pile inside. "When I look at that it seems as though we're really getting somewhere, but when I see how much more there is to move it's pretty discouraging," Peter said, after a while.

"Listen!" Sam cried. "What's that noise? Is it thunder?"

"Thunder?" Jill's heart gave a terrified leap. Would there be more rain, another flood? She strained her ears to hear. "No, it's a plane!" she cried, and they all dashed out of the cabin.

It was a plane, high and tiny against the blue sky and

moving so swiftly that it was gone almost before they saw it clearly. "Well, that's that," Greg said, in the same flat voice, leaning on his crutch and breathing heavily from his hurry.

"Do you suppose it saw our S.O.S. sign? Was it a forestry plane?" Peter asked.

"No, not a chance. From its looks and speed, it was an army jet, probably from the airfield over the mountains," Greg said. "Well, back to the salt mines, men!"

At two o'clock they had another small lunch—a piece of chocolate and some water. "How many of those bars are left?" Peter asked.

"Not very many," Jill admitted. "Just four whole ones and another small piece."

"And a can of sardines and one other big can. No one knows what's in that one," Peter said. "It's bigger than any of the others, and a different shape, too."

"Maybe it's got tennis balls in it," Sam suggested.

The others looked at him in horror. "Tennis balls!" Peter exclaimed. "What a goofy idea! Mom'd never bring a can of tennis balls up here. You know that."

"I was only kidding," Sam explained. "I read somewhere about how some people in a foreign country had this native cook. He opened a can of tennis balls and boiled them. It was real funny."

"It doesn't sound funny to *me*," Betsey said. "Tennis balls wouldn't be good to eat, even if we had a fire to cook them with, would they, Jill?"

"I should say not," Jill agreed. She had forced herself to laugh a little at Sam's joke, but as soon as she had a chance she gave the mysterious can a stealthy shake. It was very heavy and it didn't rattle or even gurgle at all. Not that I thought for a minute that it *was* tennis balls, she told herself.

Greg kept glancing outside more and more often as he worked. He's watching the sunlight, Jill thought. We haven't much time left. Unless we find the lens pretty soon, the sun won't be strong enough down here for us to use it until tomorrow.

It was nearly four o'clock by the time they had cleared away the debris from another drawer. It stuck, but Greg finally got it open—and there, at last, in a clutter of muddy, silt-soaked objects, was the camera! For a moment they all stared at it as though they couldn't believe it was real. "Golly!" Peter said, finally. "The water sure did get into it, didn't it? Do you suppose it'll take pictures, now?"

"I'm afraid not. The film's spoiled, for sure," Greg said. "But the lens is okay for our purpose, anyway."

"How are you going to get the lens out, though? I don't think it unscrews anywhere," Peter said, turning the camera over to examine it from all sides.

"I've got to get it out, Peter, even if I have to smash the camera to do it," Greg said, and held out his hand.

"Smash my camera?" Peter faltered. Greg didn't answer but continued to hold out his hand for it. After a long moment, Peter let out his breath in a sigh and gave it to him. "Okay," he said. "But—but I guess I'd rather not see you do it."

13

Sam and Betsey followed Greg outside to watch the operation, but Peter didn't go with them. He looked so forlorn that Jill stayed behind in the cabin, too. "You won't be sorry, Peter," she told him. "You'll get another camera. I'll make certain that you do, myself. That's a promise."

"It's okay," he said, but he wouldn't look at her, and the words came in a muffled whisper.

After a few minutes, Sam reappeared in the doorway. "It's all over, Pete," he announced. "Greg got it out. But he says the sun's not bright enough down here to make the lens set anything on fire. We'll have to wait until tomorrow for that. He wants us all to start gathering firewood right away, though, so we'll be ready the first thing in the morning."

Finding dry wood and bringing it in took the rest of the afternoon. Branches and logs of any size usually proved too big to move or to fit into the fireplace—for, of course, they had no axe to cut them with. "Why can't we just build our fire in the middle of the biggest sand bar?" Sam demanded, at last. "Wouldn't it be safe from spreading, there?"

Jill shook her head. "I thought of that, but then I remembered what a forest ranger told our Scout troop. Building a fire *anywhere* out in the open in the summer in the mountains is too dangerous to risk, even to try to get ourselves rescued. You know how suddenly the wind comes up sometimes. A gust could send sparks everywhere. That would be just as bad for us as the flood was—maybe worse. Building it here in the fireplace will send up just as much smoke—and it will be safe, too."

"Jill's right," Greg assured him. "Say, remember those pieces of board from the ell? They ought to be dry by now. Get all of them you can find. I can break them into lengths that'll fit."

Greg kept them at the job until what looked to Jill like an enormous pile was stacked beside the chimney. "Well, that'll have to do," he said at last, when it was almost too dark to see. "That'll keep our fire going all day, if necessary."

For supper they had sardines and water cress, which proved to be a tasty combination, and afterwards a very small bit of chocolate apiece. Jody looked so hungry and wagged his tail so pitifully that Jill gave him one of her sardines and also a crumb of her precious chocolate. He ate not only that but the paper in which it had been wrapped, licked the sardine tin thoroughly, then looked around hopefully for more. "Somebody ought to find another rattlesnake for him to eat," Sam suggested, but no one volunteered for that task.

By this time, Betsey, now buttoned into her warm red sweater, was nodding drowsily and Greg lifted her into her bunk. The twins then began to yawn, too, and, as before, climbed into their bunk of their own accord. Betsey roused herself for a moment and looked around. "I think I *might* begin to cough again if I don't have some of my medicine," she said, and Jill poured out a small dose for her.

Jill herself was tired in every muscle, but too many thoughts were racing through her mind to leave room for sleepiness. When the three children were settled, she turned to Greg. "Well, we found the lens," she said. "And we have the wood all ready, the paper too. I brought the magazines inside so the dew won't dampen them. How long do you think it will take help to get here after they see our smoke?"

"Not long. That's what fire wardens are doing all day long —watching for smoke, ready to call out a plane to locate the source. When the plane comes over it'll see your S.O.S. signal, and, if they send a helicopter, we ought to be out of here by tomorrow noon."

Jill nodded. "Yes, I guess that's right," she said, soberly, and was silent for a while. At last, in a low voice, she spoke again. "Then we'll learn the truth about Mrs. Wendell and we'll have to tell the children what's happened to their mother. Oh, Greg, I just can't bear to think of it! Honestly, I almost hate to be rescued when I know it means having to face that." There was something else in Jill's mind, too, something she didn't dare to say aloud. After we're rescued, I suppose I won't be seeing *you* again, she was thinking.

Greg had turned toward her, but she couldn't see his face in the darkness. "Well, we don't have to build the fire," he said, but she could tell by his voice that he was joking.

"Greg, you know we have to, no matter what. It's just that they're all such great kids and they've behaved so well through this whole thing. We've even had fun, in a way, at times. I simply can't stand seeing them hurt as badly as they'll have to be. That's the trouble."

"I see what you mean. Yes, it's really going to be rough," he agreed. And again there was silence in the cabin. "Look!"

he said suddenly, pointing to the doorway. "There comes the moon!"

Huge and yellow and round, it was peering over the canyon's rim. Greg hobbled to the door and Jill followed. "Let's sit down here a minute and watch it. I don't feel sleepy yet, do you?" he said.

When the moon had cleared the edge of the cliffs and was swinging free and palely silver in the sky, Greg turned to her again. This time she could see him plainly in the moon's light—blunt features and whiskery shadows and all. "It's odd you should say what you did about almost not wanting to be rescued, Jill. I was thinking the same thing myself, but for a different reason. You see I've been—well—mighty homesick ever since I left Chile last spring. Dr. Curry was nice and all, but he's—*was*—an old bachelor without any family and very few friends, so far as I could see. The man from Dad's company who's supposed to look out for me is sort of old, too. He and his wife had me to Sunday dinner several times, but their children are all married and gone.

"Well, anyway, I never managed to get acquainted with anyone at all near my age. I guess I'm sort of a shy guy, to tell the truth. There were a lot of days when I'd have given anything in the world just to be with my family—or anybody's family—for a few hours.

"Lord knows I used to gripe often enough at home about so many younger brothers and sisters always under foot, but I guess I really liked it more than I realized. Anyway, being with you four kids here—well—it's been sort of wonderful for me, short rations and sprained ankle and all. When I remembered about Dr. Curry and Mrs. Wendell I knew I oughtn't to enjoy it, really, but I couldn't help it and I can't help, either, kind of hating the thought that it'll be over so soon. It's meant a lot to me to get to know you—the twins and Betsey, too, of course—but especially you. You're quite a girl, Jill, the way you've stood up to all this. I've seen how you always manage to skimp yourself a little when you divide up the food. You're not only pretty but mighty sweet, too, and when we get out of here, I hope I'll keep on seeing you."

Jill could only sit and stare at him. Had he actually been thinking that, too? She opened her mouth to say something, but nothing would come. This miracle can't be true, she told herself. It must be a dream. If I so much as draw another breath it will all dissolve and vanish away in the moonlight.

Greg was waiting for her to speak. She could see his eyes: they looked a little anxious. "Why—why, of *course* we'll keep on seeing each other!" She spoke aloud, but her voice was small and breathless. "I want to, too. Oh, Greg, you mustn't be homesick ever again. I have a big family—not so big as yours, but nice. We have real good fun together, and I'd love to have you come in, often, any time." It wasn't a dream. He hadn't dissolved, he was still there, big and solid and kind and *terrific* as ever.

"That sounds swell. I'll take you up on that." He was smiling again, his teeth very white in his shadowed face. "Well, we have a big day ahead of us and it'll pay us to get the fire started as early as we can before the wind rises. They can see the smoke better if it goes straight up out of the canyon." His brows drew together again. "About Mrs. Wendell, Jill. There's still a chance that she's okay, you know. Things do sometimes turn out right, even if they seem hopeless. Try to think of that until we know for sure, and get some sleep."

He pulled himself up and held out his hand to her. She put hers into it and he hauled her to her feet with an easy jerk. For a moment they stood hand in hand, looking into each other's faces, while Jill felt her heart begin to pound hard against her ribs and in her ears, too. Suddenly he let go her hand, reached out and patted her cheek lightly. "Good night, Jill. Sleep tight," he said, and turned away.

Jill climbed into the bunk beside Betsey, still feeling the touch of his fingers warm on her cheek. I *will* believe that Mrs. Wendell is alive and well, somehow, somewhere, as Greg said, she declared to herself. Miracles do happen, for one has just happened to me!

Startled by the sound of Jody's barking, Jill opened her eyes and saw, to her astonishment, that it was daylight once again. Barely daylight, though, for the sun wasn't over the canyon's edge yet, and the air still felt icy cold. She climbed down as quietly as she could and hurried outside. Greg was standing by the fireplace in the old chimney busying himself at something, while Jody, having treed a squirrel, was threatening it from below.

"Hello!" he said as she joined him. "Well, this is D-Day, I guess. I'm laying the fire so it'll be ready when the sun gets here."

"Hey, you guys! How about breakfast?" It was Sam, calling from the doorway of the cabin, and a moment later Peter appeared, too.

"Golly, but it's cold," Peter said. "Are you getting the fire ready? It'd sure feel good right now."

"There, that's all set to go. Now as soon as the sun condescends to join us I can begin," Greg said, stepping back and dusting off his hands.

Already, a brilliant rim of light was spreading along the top of the cliffs, and while they watched, all but holding their breaths, a long, dazzling ray streamed down upon them. "The sun!" Jill cried, as joyfully as though it were some unexpected, blessed surprise.

Only moments later, now joined by Betsey, they were feeling its warmth on their backs as they waited in an anxious ring while Greg captured a disk of light with the lens. Carefully, he focused it on a bit of the paper under his small, carefully laid pile of fuel in the fireplace. For a long while nothing happened.

"Isn't it going to work?" Peter whispered. "After wrecking my camera and all, isn't it going to work?"

Greg didn't answer. Jill saw that he was scowling, and after a moment he licked his lips as though they had gone dry. "Isn't it going to work?" Peter asked again.

"Wait. It's too soon, yet," was all that Jill could answer, but fear was taking shape and beginning to spread coldly inside her chest. "Wait," she repeated, and gripped Peter's hand.

At long, long last, a tiny bluish shadow, thin as a thread, wavered upward and, at the same time, the tang of smoke reached their nostrils. The edges of the tiny disk of light focused on the paper turned brown, then black, then glowing red. Staring at its brilliance had so dazzled Jill's eyes that she couldn't see clearly when the first small, pale flame appeared, licked up, and caught another bit of paper, but she could smell the smoke plainly and hear a crackle as the fire met a spray of dry pine needles.

Greg fed the flame with infinite caution until there was a good, strong blaze going, then moved back. "There!" he said, and grinned triumphantly across at Jill. "There we are. I wasn't a bit sure that it would work, but it did!"

"It's making a good smoke, too," Jill said, looking up at the narrow, dark column rising into the blue sky. "Surely some firewarden somewhere is bound to see that!"

"Of course we're pretty far down in the canyon." Greg eyed the smoke with a frown. "A lot of it scatters by the time it gets high enough to be seen, and it will do that worse when the breeze comes up. Here's hoping for a windless day!"

"*Now* how about breakfast?" Sam said. "Boy, am I hungry! I'll bring out that big can."

Greg pounded the can open, but stayed close beside the fire while he worked. "I think those fresh pine needles make the most smoke," he decided, and set the others to breaking branches from the big fallen trees. Then, "Baked beans!" he announced. "Boston baked beans with pork, too. Say, this is something to cheer about!"

"And you said it would be tennis balls, Sam," Betsey reminded him.

"It was just a joke, stupid," Sam insisted. "But I'm sure glad it's beans. And such a lot of them, too!"

"More than we need for breakfast," Jill put in hastily. "After all, this is our very last can. We must save half of it for our next meal."

They ate the beans, along with more water cress. Jody ate a few beans, too, but the water cress did not interest him. Greg continued to feed the fire from the pile of fuel they had gathered the day before, adding pine branches as they were brought to him. The smoke continued to rise straight up into the bright, still air, undisturbed by any wind as yet.

"Maybe if we climbed up on top of the chimney and made smoke signals with a blanket, as the Indians did, the fire-wardens would come faster," Peter suggested.

"They'll come fast enough once they see any smoke at all," Jill assured him. "And they'll see it if it really shows above the canyon." Suddenly she had another idea. "Listen! Here's a towel apiece," she said, snatching them down from where they had been drying. "If a plane comes over we must all of us begin to wave towels as hard as we can."

"What for? They'll see our signal and the S.O.S." Sam protested. "That ought to be enough to tell them we want help."

"If we're all out waving something white, they'll be able to count us, to know how many of us there are," Jill explained.

148

Peter nodded eagerly. "Then they'll know how many helicopters to send," he agreed.

They practiced standing in a row and waving the towels, while the fire crackled and the sun grew hotter and hotter. "Well, there's no use in getting sunstrokes," Greg said, at last. "We might as well sit in the shade while we wait." He piled more of the green pine branches on the blaze and they all moved into the cooler shadow of the willows. "What time is it, Jill?"

"Nine-thirty. The fire's been going over an hour," she told him.

"That long? And the wind usually comes up about ten o'clock," he said, looking questioningly at the sky. "I sure hope it stays away for a while later, today."

It was Jody who caught the sound first. He had been lying in the shade beside Jill, allowing her to scratch a special place under his chin, when he suddenly pricked up his ears. An instant later, the others heard it, too. "A plane!" Jill cried, jumping to her feet. "Get the towels!"

Frantically, they rushed out into the open just as the aircraft appeared. It was a helicopter, moving slowly, halting in the air, then hovering directly above them while its noise filled the canyon. "There's two people in it!" Sam shouted above the din.

"Oh, maybe one of them's Mommy!" Betsey cried, and at the sight of her happy, eager face Jill felt a pang even in her joy and excitement.

"No, they're both men—rangers," Peter said.

"Come, we must get out of the way while they land," Jill said, grabbing Betsey's hand.

Slowly the helicopter settled to the earth, its whirling blades grew still, and a uniformed ranger jumped out. "It's Jim! It's our own ranger, Jim!" Sam cried, running to greet him. "Hi, Jim! Boy, are we glad to see you!"

Jim was staring at them with a strange expression. "You're really the Wendells, aren't you? Sure, I'm mighty glad to see you too, of course. But how in the world did you kids get back up here?"

"*Back* up here?" Jill echoed. "Why, we've been right here ever since the flood. We couldn't get out."

"You weren't in the car with Mrs. Wendell at all, then?" He still looked at them in amazement. "Ever since she began to regain consciousness a little she's been calling for you. We thought, of course, you had been in the station wagon with her and had all been swept away by the flood and—well, we've been searching for you downstream all this while!"

"Then—then she's *alive!*" Jill cried, still hardly daring to believe what he seemed to be telling them. "She's alive? She's all right, after all?"

"She's alive and she's going to be all right, but she's still in the hospital and not quite herself. Her car was turned over several times by the water and she got some bad bruises and a concussion. She still can't remember what happened, but she's beginning to come out of it."

"Mom in the hospital?" Peter's freckled face looked scared. "What is a con— a concussion?"

"It's a bad bump on the head," Jim explained. "But don't worry. The doctors say she's going to be fine before very long. Especially when she learns that you're all safe and sound! Let's see, you must be Jill Gray? And you?" He looked at Greg. "We want to radio the news right away."

"I'm Greg Murdoch. I was with Dr. Curry. How about him? Is he—?" Greg asked.

The ranger's face sobered and he shook his head. "I'm sorry. We found his body down below. We were looking for you there, too, as a matter of fact."

"Oh Greg!" Jill said, turning to him. "I'm so sorry. He was your friend. I was really trying to hope—"

Greg shook his head. "No, I knew that he hadn't had a chance when I saw him swept away. But—" he broke off. "He was such a nice old guy!" he added, his voice suddenly a little hoarse.

The ranger spoke again, breaking the momentary silence. "Well, in spite of that, this is ending up a lot better than any of us dared to hope for. Now let's see about lifting you out of here. It'll take two trips."

"Boy, oh boy!" Sam cried. "Can we get in right now?" he was leaping forward when Peter grabbed him by the arm.

"What's the matter with you, Sam? Don't you remember? It's always women and children first," he said. "Take Betsey and Jill, Jim. Me and Greg and Sam'll wait for the second trip."

The ranger's eyes twinkled a little, but he answered Peter gravely. "That's the right idea, usually, but this time I think we can take all of you youngsters at once," he said. "Greg and I can wait behind to make sure that the fire is out. I want to have a look around the area, too, so that I can make a report."

"But Greg's ankle. It really needs a doctor right away," Jill had found her voice at last enough to protest. "I can stay and help you put out the fire. Send him on the first trip."

Greg refused to hear of such a thing, however, and the twins, Betsey, Jill, and Jody, too, were boosted aboard the helicopter. Jill looked out at Greg leaning on his crutch beside the ranger, as the engine began to roar again. Greg waved, and then, as the craft rose slowly into the air, he formed a circle with his forefinger and thumb, smiled, and nodded to her. Quickly, she responded with the same gesture.

"I'll take you to the ranger station," Frank, the pilot, said when they were out of the canyon and soaring over the rugged slopes of the mountain. "Dr. Wendell and your father, Jill, and your brother, too, are all with the search party, digging down below in the new channel that the flood made. I'll call them in right away. This is sure the sort of news it's a pleasure to broadcast."

Then Frank, speaking into his microphone, sent the message out over the airwaves that the three Wendell children, together with Jill Gray and Greg Murdoch, who had all been given up for lost in the flood, were found alive and well. Jill listened, struggling to bring her mind to a realization of what those words of his meant. She had been so very sure that the reason no help had come for them was the single tragic one: that Mrs. Wendell had been trapped and drowned in the canyon, and that therefore no one knew of their plight. Least of all her own family!

Now, with a jarring shock, full understanding overwhelmed her. Pictures began to flash through her head like views in a kaleidoscope. Her father and Rick with the search party hunting down in the rubble that the flood had left—hunting —*digging*, the pilot had said. Hunting for her body! Her mother and Beth waiting for news. Her family, who loved her so much, thinking her dead all this while. Phoebe, too— poor Phoebe, who would feel that somehow she was to blame. A searing pain filled her throat.

"Why Jill, are you crying? Whatever are you crying for, when we're being rescued, and in a helicopter, too?" she heard Betsey exclaim.

"I—I don't know," was all that Jill could answer. "But I know I'll be all right in just a minute."

14

Jill had managed to regain her composure by the time the helicopter began to descend over the ranger station. Peering out, Jill saw that there were a number of cars and trucks parked around the open field on which they were landing. Jill and the three young Wendells were no sooner helped to the ground by a uniformed sheriff than they were surrounded by a crowd of men who began to focus cameras and flashbulbs in their faces. "The reporters got here fast, I see," the pilot said.

All the men were smiling and friendly, but they kept shouting at the children, calling them by name, telling them to turn this way and that, until the commotion frightened Betsey. She turned away and hid her face against Jill, while the twins, too, looked a little daunted.

While Jill stood holding Betsey to her in momentary bewilderment, she caught sight of Rick fighting his way through the throng. He was wearing the broadest grin she had ever seen on his face, and the hug he gave her when he reached her at last squeezed most of the breath out of her. Then it was her father who held her close, close, as though he never wanted to let her go. "Jill, baby. Little Jill!" he kept saying over and over.

When he released her at last, Jill saw him reach for his handkerchief, mop his eyes, and blow his nose, and so she began to cry a little, herself, but these were joyful tears that didn't hurt at all.

Professor Wendell was there with them, too, trying to gather all three of his children into his arms at once. Another familiar voice called Jill's name. She turned in a sort of happy daze, blinking through wet lashes, and saw, to her astonishment, that it was Rod Campbell. Like Rick's, his clothes were stained with mud. He was in the search party, too, Jill thought. That was *nice* of him. He really is handsome—almost too handsome, she found herself deciding. Why, he's sort of *pretty*. For Greg's rugged face was still filling her mind.

Now the helicopter was taking off again, and the ranger's wife had her arm around Jill and was drawing her through the crowd toward the house. "Let the child through, boys," she told the reporters and photographers. "I've called the good news down to her mother, and she's waiting on the phone to speak to her, herself."

Her mother's voice over the wire sounded strange and choked, at first, but it soon became comfortably familiar and dear, as Jill assured her that she was well and unharmed. There didn't seem to be much else that her mother wanted to hear except just that, again and again. "Yes, I really am all right," Jill kept telling her. "And so are the children. No, I wasn't alone with them all the time. There was this boy named Greg Murdoch, he was caught in the flood, too, and he joined us the next day. Even though he had a sprained ankle, he helped us all so much. If it hadn't been for him—!

Yes, Mother, honestly I'm all right. Sort of hungry and terribly dirty, but really and truly okay. And, oh, I love you, Mother!"

Then Beth wanted to talk to Jill, and then her father wished to speak to their mother and Jill handed him the phone. When he had finished, the ranger's wife, whose name was Mollie, reappeared and took them into her kitchen, where the three young Wendells were already feasting on milk and sandwiches. Yes, peanut butter sandwiches, Jill found herself noticing! And Jody, too, was busy with a bowl of something under the table.

Professor Wendell was sitting between the twins with Betsey enthroned on his lap. One of the sheriff's men, aided by Rick and Rod, was guarding the door against the crowd of reporters and photographers who still seemed to want to take more pictures and ask more questions. "Give these hungry kids a chance. When they've a little something inside them, I'll let you talk to them again," the officer was saying.

"Hi, Jill!" Peter called to her. "I've been telling my dad how fast you hustled us up that trail ahead of the flood. You really did save our lives, you know."

"Yes, and you really brought our basket of lunch along, even if you spilled the milk," Betsey added. "And you dug cans of food out of the mud for us when our kitchen got washed away, and you hit the rattlesnake with a rock when he tried to bite me, and then Greg killed it and cut off its head and Jody had it for his dinner because there wasn't any more dog food."

"But it was Greg who got Sam down off the cliff when he got stuck halfway up," Peter reminded them. "And it was Greg who figured out about building a fire by using my camera lens when we didn't have any matches. That's how we signaled for help."

There was so much to explain that nobody knew where to

begin and everybody interrupted everyone else, but the only thing that really mattered to anyone was that they were safe. Mrs. Wendell, also, would soon be well and home from the hospital, Jill learned from the professor. Meanwhile, the children's grandmother had been sent for and she would be there to look after them all when they reached home.

The ranger's wife served Jill milk and sandwiches, too, but even while she was savoring the indescribably delicious fare, she was listening for the sound of the helicopter coming back, for it would be bringing Greg to join them.

When it had come at last and he had made his way through the crowd to them, had been welcomed, and introduced to everyone and was sitting at the table beside her, eating and drinking too, it seemed to Jill that the world had never been so bright and beautiful as at this instant.

"So you were with Dr. Curry?" Professor Wendell said to Greg. "I didn't know him personally, but I knew his work. He was a fine scientist."

"He was very good to me," Greg said, and for a moment sadness clouded the cheerful little room.

Jill's father spoke up briskly. "Well, Greg, you'll need another place to stay when we all get back to town. Suppose you come along home with us. I want our doctor to look at that ankle of yours right away."

"Why, that's mighty nice of you, sir. I'd sure like to—if I won't be too much trouble," Greg said.

And then Rick, who could be maddening but could also be the most wonderful brother in the world, reached over and slapped Greg's shoulder. "Trouble? After all you've done? I've got plenty of space in my room. You can move right in with me, Greg. Say, that ought to make us a balanced family at last—you and me and Beth and Jelly Bean, here."

Jelly Bean! All the grateful warmth Jill had felt within her for Rick changed to hot rage. She could feel it rising in her cheeks. How could he call her that hateful name now, and in front of Greg, too?

"Jelly Bean?" Greg was repeating. He turned in his chair and looked down at her, smiling. "So that's what they call you? It's a real cute name—I always did like jelly beans—but I guess I like just 'Jill' better. Okay if I keep on calling you that, still?"

"It's okay," Jill told him. Even as she spoke, she was thinking that "Jelly Bean," the way he said it, sounded sort of nice, after all.